LOYALTY

TO A

GANGSTA

J. L. Rose

GOOD2GO PUBLISHING

LOYALTY TO A GANGSTA
Written by J. L. Rose
Cover Design: Davida Baldwin
Typesetter: Mychea
ISBN: 9781947340039
Copyright ©2017 Good2Go Publishing
Published 2017 by Good2Go Publishing
7311 W. Glass Lane • Laveen, AZ 85339
www.good2gopublishing.com
https://twitter.com/good2gobooks
G2G@good2gopublishing.com
www.facebook.com/good2gopublishing
www.instagram.com/good2gopublishing

ACKNOWLEDGMENTS

This book is for my fans!
We doing it big, family!
Let's take a ride!

DEDICATION

This book is dedicated first to my Heavenly Father and then to my mother and father. Without the three of you, who and where would I be? I hope I'm making you three proud.

LOYALTY TO A GANGSTA

PROLOGUE

Nicole checked her watch for probably the fifth time while waiting in the lobby of Miami International Airport. She was waiting for her husband's son, who she knew about; however, she had never met him and only saw pictures that his son's mother had sent to her husband through the mail. Nicole found herself remembering the near divorce she and her husband almost went through because of the same woman and the child who now was coming to live with them, after the death of the young man's mother.

Nicole ignored any further thoughts about the past and noticed that the lobby was filling as passengers were exiting the plane that had just landed. She heard the announcement over the intercom and stood from her seat when she recognized the flight number.

She began to look around, searching for the face she had seen many times in photos her husband had received. Her husband never really looked at these photos; instead, he simply put them away in the back of the desk drawer in his home office. Nicole slowly walked through the crowded lobby and continued to look around. She almost missed the face she was seeking out, had the young man not looked the way he did while standing just a few feet away. He was standing with a cute young woman who looked maybe only three or four years older this his seventeen years.

Nicole was shocked and surprised at how amazingly handsome her husband's son was. He stood five foot ten and weighed 192 pounds, and was lean and athletic with a nicely muscular frame. She stood waiting a few minutes until the young lady walked off, and then the young man looked up directly at Nicole.

"Jesus!" she whispered after meeting his gorgeous hazel eyes.

Nicole started toward him and then stopped in front of him.

"Hi! I'm Nicole."

"I figured that since you stood staring and waiting either for me or the girl," he stated before asking, "So, where's Dwayne?"

"He, ummmm! He's handling an issue," Nicole told him. "Do you have any other bags?"

"Yeah!" he replied with a small smirk on his face.

Gabriel picked up his bags from baggage claim and then headed toward the exit. Nicole led the young man out to her M5 BMW and hit the car locks by remote. She walked around to the driver's side as the young man walked up to the passenger side and put his bags onto the back seat.

Once they were inside the car and her husband's son was seated beside her, Nicole backed out the M5 from its parking spot and pulled off. She then glanced over at the young man and saw him silently staring out the window.

"Gabriel, right?" she asked, seeing him nod his head while continuing to stare out the window.

Nicole made another attempt to talk to Gabriel, only to receive silence in return. She respected the fact that maybe he didn't want to talk and just focused on the road once more.

"He doesn't want me here, do he? Dwayne, I mean?" he finally spoke up.

"Why would you ask that, Gabriel?" Nicole asked, a little surprised at his question.

"We both know Dwayne's not handling anything. He just didn't want to come, and he really didn't want me coming here. But it's cool! I've already heard about how he feels about me from my grandfather," he replied with a light laugh as he cut his eyes over to Nicole.

Nicole was unsure of what to say, and was only able to look over at the young man as he was once again staring out the window. Nicole remained silent and focused on driving them home— his new home or what she hoped would turn out to be his home.

Present Day

G abe got his first look of how his father was living after riding through the upper-class neighbor-hood. He sat staring out the front passenger window at the two-story white and royal blue house which grew closer as Nicole drove onto the driveway and parked in front of the two-car garage. He climbed from the car and glanced over at the S-Class Mercedes-Benz that was parked right next to them as he grabbed his bags from the back seat.

Gabe walked around the back end of the BMW after picking up his bag and met up with Nicole, who stood waiting for him. The two of them then walked together up to the front door in silence.

"Nice S-Class!" Gabe stated, breaking the silence after Nicole opened the front door.

Gabe then walked into the house, leaving Nicole standing at the door behind him. She then followed him inside the house. Once they were inside, Nicole locked the front door and then headed toward the den, since the television could be heard playing. She found her husband on the sofa wearing his reading glasses with the papers laid out in front of him on top of the coffee table while CNN played on the TV.

"David!" Nicole called, getting her husband's attention.

"Hey!" David replied, glancing over and accepting the kiss his wife gave him after she walked over.

He pulled off his glasses and tossed them onto the coffee table.

"So, what happened? The bastard decided not to come after all?"

"David!" Nicole cried out in warning, glancing back in the direction where his son was looking at family photos and not paying attention to their conversation. She looked back at her husband.

"He's right out in the front! He's just looking at the pictures, David!" Nicole said in a lowered voice.

"So, the bastard actually came, huh?" David asked as he sat back in the sofa. "You told him what was expected?"

"He doesn't talk much!" she mentioned. "I

tried talking to him in the car. He said a few words, but mostly he was quiet."

"I hope the boy stays that way," he told Nicole as he sat forward and picked up his glasses again.

"Aren't you going to talk to him?" Nicole asked, seeing her husband getting back to his paper.

"For what?" David asked, looking back at Nicole. "What do I have to say to the bastard? You're the one who agreed to deal with him!"

Nicole sucked her teeth at her husband and then rolled her eyes as she turned and left the den. She found Gabriel standing at the back sliding-glass door looking out over the backyard.

"Gabriel!"

Gabe turned around at the sound of his name and saw Nicole alone and approaching him. He stood where he was as she stopped in front of him.

"David says he'll see you later after you get settled in and he's finished with his work. You want me to show you to your new room?" she asked him with a small smile.

Gabe nodded his head in response, picked up his bags, and then followed Nicole from the front room and started up the stairs.

* * *

Gabe got a brief look around as Nicole led the way to his new bedroom that was located at the far end of the back of the hall, away from the other bedrooms. He wasn't surprised at what he saw when he entered the mid-size bedroom. It had little inside of it other than a twin bed, two dressers, and a small fold-out table that sat in the corner at the head of the bed.

"Gabriel—!"

"Thanks!" Gabe stated, cutting off Nicole in a dismissive tone of voice.

Nicole heard the way Gabriel had thanked her, and watched him begin to unpack in silence. She simply backed out of the bedroom and shut the door behind her as she left.

Gabe heard the click from the door after she left. He shook his head and continued to unpack, but he soon found himself smirking as he replayed the conversation he heard only a few minutes ago between Nicole and his father.

Gabe hung up and put away his things, and then he sat at the foot of the bed. He just sat and thought for a few minutes of how he was going to deal with a father who didn't know him and who really didn't want to deal with him. He soon found himself thinking about his mother, but he had to kill the thought before he got upset again.

He stood from the bed and walked out of his bedroom and downstairs. Nicole and his father were talking loud enough that he could hear them. He then headed straight for the front door and was just unlocking it when he heard his name from behind him. He looked back over his shoulder to see Nicole standing at the entrance to the den.

"Yeah!"

"Where are you going?" she asked as she started toward him.

"Just going for a walk," he told her as he then opened the front door and stepped out of the house.

He walked toward the sidewalk and saw Nicole still watching him from the front door. He then headed up the street. He just started to walk, unsure exactly where he was going, since this was his first time in Miami.

* * *

Gabe was unsure how far or how long he was walking, but he came up to a mom-and-pop store on the corner. He went inside and bought an orange soda, a box of Newports, and a brand-new lighter. He ignored the look given to him from the man behind the counter when he asked for the

5

cigarettes. After he walked out of the store, he noticed a park a few blocks up the street. He began walking toward the park and saw a nice-sized crowd playing basketball as he got closer.

Gabe cut through the parking lot, walked over to the bleachers, and found a spot by himself to watch the game that was going on. He opened the Newports and dug out a cigarette. After firing one up and leaning back against the rail behind him, he sat watching the basketball game while ignoring the whispering and staring coming from the females at the bottom of the bleachers.

Gabe heard some commotion all of a sudden to his left and saw three dudes who circled around a brown-skinned kid with cornrows in his head. He sat and watched the show for a few moments, but then shook his head, looked away, and focused back on the basketball game. But the game had now come to a halt, as the players were more interested in the four young men.

* * *

"Muthafucker! You think I'm playing about my money, don't you?" Duke heard the nigga, TEC-9, yelling while trying his hardest to catch everyone's attention out on the basketball court to put on a show.

Duke didn't bother with responding or going back and forth with the clown in front of him. Instead, he kept a close eye on the rest of TEC-9's boys who had surrounded him. He shook his head and tried to leave, when TEC-9 decided to shove him back into the middle of the circle in which he was crowded.

Duke reacted on impulse, and slung the basket-ball he held in his hands straight at TEC-9's face. Duke rushed in behind the ball and was able to catch TEC-9 with a right to the face. Then the rest of TEC-9's boys fell in on him. He fought back as hard as he could, catching a few of their asses when he was hit to the back of the head, which dazed him. Duke felt himself fall to one knee, and all he could do was ball up as the blows began running down on him.

Duke felt the blows suddenly stop, but he heard the fight still going on. He then looked up to see a light-skinned kid going to work on TEC-9 and his boys all by himself. He jumped up and rushed to go help the dude who was helping him. Duke ran up on one of TEC-9's boys and scooped his ass up from the back and slammed his ass on his head.

Duke ignored the dude's screams after

dumping him on his head. He then got back in the fight as both he and Gabe got in some work until TEC-9 and his homeboys broke out and ran away.

Duke watched as TEC-9 and his punk-ass homeboys made good time running away from the basketball court and across the parking lot. He then turned back to the homeboy who had just helped him out.

"What's ya name, my nigga?"

"Gabe!" he answered as he turned to walk off.

"Hold up!" Duke called out, grabbing Gabe's arm. "Everybody calls me Duke. But I think we need to leave. The fool we just got at has a brother that traps a few blocks from here, and if I know Tec-o, the nigga is going to holla at his brother."

Gabe agreed to leave with Duke as the both of them took off jogging from the park, into the parking lot, and into a dark blue Explorer. Duke unlocked the SUV and both he and Gabe got in.

Duke pulled out of the parking lot a minute later and sped away from the park.

"I ain't say it back at the park, but good looking out with having my back. I owe you," Duke said.

"You good, playboy!" Gabe told him. "You don't owe me nothing!"

Duke nodded his head and showed a small smile.

"So, where you from? You got an accent to ya' voice," he asked Gabe.

"That's because I'm half Dominican and black!" Gabriel explained. "I'm from Chicago though."

"You far from home!" Duke stated. "You visiting family down here in Miami?"

"Something like that!" Gabe said, shaking his head and thinking about his father and the house in which he was now living.

2

G abe rode with Duke and asked no questions about where they were going, since he was in no real hurry to get back to his father's house. Gabe sat inside the Explorer once they pulled in front of a house in the Opa-locka area, at which Duke had explained they would stop. Gabe then let down his window a crack and dug out a Newport.

Duke left Gabe in the SUV as he walked up to his girlfriend's house. He then stepped up onto the porch and knocked on the front door, only to hear a woman yell from inside the house asking who it was.

"It's Duke, Ms. Jackson!"

"Hey, baby!" Ms. Jackson said, smiling after opening the front door and seeing her daughter's boyfriend at the door. "How you doing, Duke?"

"I'm fine, Ms. Jackson. Is Melody here?"

"You just missed her, baby. She just left with her friends to walk to that girl Gina's house. If you leave now, you may be able to catch her."

"Thanks, Ms. Jackson."

Duke jogged back out to the Explorer and hopped in behind the wheel. He pulled off and headed up the street in the direction of Gina's house.

"You smoke?" Gabe asked, holding out the pack of Newports.

"No doubt!" Duke stated as he took the pack. "How old is you, my nigga?"

"Seventeen!"

"You had me thinking you was older. You don't act like someone seventeen."

"So I've been told!" Gabe replied as he took the Newports box that Duke had handed back to him.

* * *

"Melody!" Gina cried out as she and her girls sat out on the front porch of her house. "Girl, your boyfriend's coming!"

Melody turned her head to the left to see Duke's truck driving up the street. She smiled as she sat watching the Ford Explorer as it pulled to a stop in front of Gina's house.

"Girl, who is that in the car with Duke?" Michelle asked, also staring over at the Explorer.

"I don't know!" Melody answered, seeing the boy in the passenger seat of Duke's truck.

She stepped off the porch as Duke walked up.

"What's up?" Duke said as he walked up on Melody and kissed her on the lips.

"What you doing over here?" Melody asked him as she reached up to rub his freshly done corn rolls, only to pause when she felt the knot on his head, which caused him to hiss.

She grabbed Duke and turned him around to see the knot at the back of his head.

"Duke! What the hell happened to your head?"

"It's nothing!"

"Boy, don't play with me, Duke!" she told him. "What happened to your head?"

Duke sighed as he rubbed the back of his head, and then he told Melody about the fight at the park. He also told her about how Gabe had helped him.

"Who the hell is Gabe?" Melody asked as she threw her hands up onto her hips.

Duke nodded back at the Explorer and then turned and called out to Gabe, waving him out of the truck.

Melody looked past Duke and saw the cream-complexioned boy who climbed from the Explorer. She heard her girls behind her, but she too had to admit that whoever this Gabe guy was, he was fine as hell.

"Yo, Gabe! This is my lady, Melody," Duke introduced the two.

"What up, shorty?" Gabe said, speaking first.

"So, you're the one that helped my man out, huh?" Melody stated, looking Gabe over.

She began to say more, only to be interrupted as her girls rushed up, with Gina getting to Gabe first.

"Damn, baby. Who is you and where is your woman?" Gina asked as she boldly looked Gabe over.

She ran her hand down Gabe's chest and was at his mid-section and moving lower when Melody grabbed her and pulled her away.

"Gina, girl. Stop!" Melody said, shaking her head, but noticing the small smile on Gabe's lips. "You need to take your ass in the house and take a cold shower."

"That ain't what I need!" Gina said, blowing a kiss at Gabe.

"Anyways!" Melody began, rolling her eyes at Gina before looking back at Duke and Gabe. "So what you two about to do?"

"I was going to pick you up and take you with me back to the house. But I'ma slide with Gabe a little bit. You going to the twins' party tonight, right?" Duke asked.

"What time we leaving?" Melody asked.

But before Duke could answer, she looked at

Gabe and was just about to ask him if he was coming to the party, only to see him walk off.

"Gabe! Where you going?"

Gabe walked over to the driveway of Melody's homegirl's house and stopped beside the car that he easily recognized, even though the thing had paint peeling off of it and the convertible top had holes in it.

"Yo, Duke!" Gabe called out as he continued looking over the car.

"What's up, my nigga?" Duke said as he and the girls walked over to stand beside Gabe.

"Ask you lady!"

"I'm right here, Gabe!" Melody spoke up, cutting him off. "You can ask me yourself!"

Gabe looked from the car over at Melody and said, "I just wanted you to get at whichever one of ya girls whose house this is. I want to ask her if they're selling this car."

"You can ask me yourself, baby daddy!" Gina stated as she walked up to Gabe's left side and wrapped her arms around his waist.

Gabe was unable to not smirk at Gina.

"What's up, shorty? Whose ride this is?"

"It was my mom's until she got a new car!" Gina told him. "Why you asking? You want it or something?"

14

"Find out what your mom wants for it for me, shorty," Gabe told her.

"She gonna tell me to let you have it!" Gina told him. "She's been meaning to call the junkyard and have them come and get the thing, but I'll call her now if you want me to."

"Yeah! Check on that for me, shorty," Gabe told her, watching as she took off running toward the front door to the house.

* * *

Gabe left Gina's house and had Duke follow behind him as he drove the old 1974 Chevy Caprice convertible that he basically got for free. He only had to promise to take Gina out on a date after her mother all but begged him to take the drop-top Caprice. Gabe ignored the wet mold smell and even the light smoking coming from beneath the hood. He made it back to his father's house after the car shut off twice on him a few minutes from the house.

He parked the Caprice out in front of the house and climbed out from inside the car, only to hear his name. He looked up to see Nicole and two young-looking dudes with her at the front door.

"Gabriel, whose car is that?" Nicole asked him as he entered the front yard while staring at the piece of junk that was now sitting in front of her house.

"It's mine!" Gabe answered as he walked up onto the porch and saw two young boys. "Who are the two youngin's, Nicole?"

"Youngin's?" one of the two boys spoke up with an attitude as the two of them stepped toward Gabe.

"Kyle! Aaron! This is Gabriel!" Nicole spoke up.

"So, this is David's bastard?" Aaron asked with a smirk.

"Aaron!" Nicole yelled, shooting her oldest son a look, only for Gabe to begin chuckling and drawing her attention back to him.

"I see my father has been talking about me again!" Gabe said with a smile. "I'm impressed, but I hope to get the chance to meet both of your boys' fathers!"

Gabe saw the look that appeared on Nicole's face as well as on the faces of both her sons. He continued smiling as he walked by the three of them into the house. Gabe headed straight to his room upstairs and heard Nicole call out to him. He kept walking until he got into his room as he heard Nicole enter behind him.

"Gabriel!" Nicole called out as she spotted

him standing at his closet. "What is your problem? Was that necessary back at the front door?"

"You should be asking them sons of yours, since we both know who opened the door for the bullshit!" Gabe told her as he walked past her to lay his clothes across the twin bed. "Are you even concerned or just in here because you're really into defending your sons?"

Nicole sighed deeply as she stood watching Gabe pack up some clothes. She folded her arms across her chest.

"Where are you going, Gabriel?" she asked.

"I was invited to a party," Gabe told her as he was packing his backpack. "I'll be back late, or should I just find someplace else to sleep until morning?"

"I'll have a key for you before you leave, Gabriel."

"I'm leaving now!" he told her while picking up his clothes and the backpack.

"Come on!" Nicole told him as she turned and left the bedroom, leading Gabe to her and David's bedroom.

* * *

"So Aaron and his little brother, Kyle, are your step-brothers, huh?" Duke asked, after

17

pulling off from in front of Gabe's house.

Gabe shook his head at the way Nicole had approached him and defended her two soft-ass sons.

"Yeah! They my pop's step-sons. I ain't got too much of nothing to do with 'em!" Gabe answered Duke.

"That's mostly how people at the school treat they ass too!" Duke stated, shaking his head. "The nigga Aaron tried to holla at my sister and got his feelings hurt."

"You got a sister?"

"Yeah! But she sometimes acts more like my brother than my sister."

"Ain't nothing wrong with that!"

"We'll see if you say that same shit when you see her ass!"

Gabe nodded his head as he turned to look out the window, just as old-school Trick Daddy Dollars came blaring through the speakers. Gabe began nodding his head to the *Book of Thugs* that was banging through the car.

3

Shantae was hanging out in front of the house with Boo Man and Silk. They were smoking and listening to Rick Ross blaring from the sound system inside a Ford F-150. Shantae looked up at the sound of a car pulling up, only to see her brother Duke's Ford Explorer pulling alongside her. She hit the blunt she held once more and then passed it over to Silk before pushing off the fence from in front of the F-150.

"Where you just coming from?" Shantae called out to her brother, but paused when she noticed somebody else climbing out from inside his truck.

"What's up, Shantae?" Duke said as he and Gabe got out of the Explorer.

He nodded to Boo Man and Silk as they walked up, who then both looked back at Shantae staring hard at Gabe.

"Shantae, this is my nigga Gabe! Gabe, this is my bro, I mean, my sister, Shantae!"

"Keep playing, nigga!" Shantae said, sucking her teeth as she punched Duke in the chest.

She then looked back at Gabe and met his eyes as he stood staring at her. "You plan on saying something, nigga, or just staring at me?"

"I'd rather look than talk, ma! You miss more by running ya mouth, and right now, I'm kinda feeling what I'm seeing!" Gabe replied with a slow smirk.

"What, nigga?" Shantae yelled, more out of surprise than anger at what she just heard. "Dude, you trying to get your player shit on?"

"I don't do the playing game, ma!" Gabe told her in all seriousness. "When I say something, it's what it is. Period!"

"Where you from, homeboy?" Silk spoke up as he slid up beside Shantae and stared hard at the nigga Gabe.

"Chi-Town!" Gabe answered the slightly heavy-set brown-skinned dude with the blunt. "Big homie, you selling some more of that?"

"Naw, Chi-Town!" Boo Man answered just as Shantae spoke up again as she took the blunt out of his hand. "What you trying to get, nigga?"

"You got it, ma?" Gabe asked, turning back to look at her.

"Nigga, what I just ask you?" Shantae asked with a forced attitude.

She barely had time to react as Gabe's hand reached out and grabbed her by the back of her neck with just enough force and gentleness. She found herself pulled over to within a few inches of him, and she could smell his cologne as he leaned in and whispered into her ear.

Duke watched Gabe with his sister and wondered what he was whispering to her. But he saw the way she was loosely holding onto his hand that was holding the back of her neck. Duke was surprised when Shantae slowly nodded her head and then dug inside her pocket and pulled out two thick bags of weed. She then handed them over to Gabe, who handed her some money in return.

"You smoking with me, right, ma?" Gabe asked as he stood staring into Shantae's brown eyes.

"Naw!" Silk spoke up, drawing everybody but Gabe's attention toward him. "She got some business to handle with me and Boo Man!"

"Maybe later then!" Gabe told Shantae, seeing her give a nod as she stepped around him to follow Silk and Boo Man.

Gabe smiled as he watched Shantae walk off but turn around to look back at him before climbing into the F-150.

Duke then tapped Gabe's arm and asked,

"You the only dude I ever saw her react to like that! What the fuck did you say to her just now?"

"I just asked her to sell me some weed!" Gabe admitted, telling only half the truth while staring at the F-150 as it drove off.

* * *

Gabe met Ms. Mitchell, Duke and Shantae's mother, and their step-father, Mr. James. He then sat down and talked with Duke's parents a little while, until first Mr. James received a visitor at the house and then the house phone rang and got Ms. Mitchell's attention. Duke rushed Gabe out of the front room and back into his bedroom, away from his mother and step-father.

"Sorry about that, my nigga!" Duke apologized. "My mom loves talking, and my step-dad's right along with her."

"Your mom seems cool!" Gabe stated as he was looking around Duke's bedroom at the different pictures that hung on the walls.

"Yo, check it though!" Duke stated as he walked over to his closet. "If you plan on showering, you can go ahead and go first. I'ma jump in behind you. We leaving here by seven to pick up Melody and Gina."

"What's up with Shantae?" Gabe asked

without looking over at Duke. "Ma going to this party too?"

Duke smiled at the question Gabe had just asked him about his sister. He then patted his boy on his back.

"Yeah! She's going. But let me help you out now, my nigga. If you thinking about getting at her, don't! Shantae's not the normal type of female you're probably used to kicking it with!"

"I hear you!" Gabe replied, even though he really wasn't paying the boy no damn attention.

* * *

Shantae got back to the house a little after six. She planned to be ready by seven thirty, by the time Silk and Boo Man returned to the house to pick her up for the party for the twins that night. She entered the front door and could smell her mother's cooking, so she stopped in the kitchen to see food wrapped up but on top of the stove. She looked inside the different pots and pans at what her mother had put together, grabbing a fried chicken wing before leaving.

As Shantae headed for the back of the house toward her bedroom, she heard "All Eyez on Me" banging from behind her brother's bedroom door. She walked straight into Duke's bedroom and froze right at the door and stared.

"You plan on standing there and staring, ma?" Gabe asked her with a smirk.

Shantae heard him but watched the black metallic jeans he intentionally pulled slowly up his thighs. She couldn't help noticing the size of the print that pressed against the front of his boxers before disappearing behind the jeans. She shifted her eyes up to his hard six-pack stomach and then continued upward to his chest. She saw the tattoo right-side piece that covered his right chest and a half sleeve on his right arm. She finally met his eyes once she stopped staring at his chest. By this time, Shantae was thinking of doing things that had her mouth watering.

"Umm! Am I interrupting?" Duke asked, causing Shantae to jump in surprise.

He walked into the bedroom with a smile as he passed her at the door.

"What's up, Shantae?"

"I, ummm! Boo Man asked me to, ummm. He said he got what you wanted," Shantae was able to get out of her mouth, while still staring at Gabe, who was now sitting shirtless at the foot of Duke's bed putting on a pair of brown Timberlands.

"Yeah, a'ight, Shantae!" Duke stated. When his sister was still at the door staring at Gabe, he yelled, "Shantae! Leave!"

Gabe smiled a little bit as Shantae finally left the bedroom, slamming the door behind her. Gabe looked at a smiling Duke who stood shaking his head and staring back at him.

* * *

Duke and Gabe were dressed and left the house a little after 7:00. They arrived at Melody's by 7:20 and then at Gina's by 7:29. They then all had to wait another ten minutes until Gina brought her ass out of the house.

"Hey, y'all!" Gina said as she climbed into the back seat with Gabe. She broke into a smile when she saw him. "Hey, baby daddy!"

"What up, Gina?" Gabe replied as he passed the blunt he was smoking back up front to Duke.

Duke made one more stop at the store at the request of Melody and Gina, and then they finally drove to Opa-locka where the birthday party was being held. Duke turned down the street on which the twins lived, only to see the street and front yard completely crowded with partygoers. Once Duke found a place to park and the four of them got out of his Explorer, Gina quickly wrapped her arm around Gabe's waist. She then broke into a big smile when he laid his arm across her shoulders.

"Duke!" Melody called. "Baby, ain't that Silk's truck right there?"

Duke looked to where his girl was pointing and spotted the F-150. Duke nodded his head and told Melody that it was indeed Silk's truck, just as somebody yelled out his name. He turned around to see a few people he knew and threw up his hands in response.

Once at the party and slowly making it through the front yard, and being stopped every few minutes by different people, Duke, Melody, and Gina talked to some of their friends. At the same time, numerous females stepped up to Gabe and tried to talk to him, until Gina interrupted every time and gave each of them attitude. Once they were inside the house that was just as crowded, Melody found the twins, Shanna and Shana, and gave them their birthday presents from her and Duke.

"Does he come with the gift too?" Shana asked while smirking at Gabe.

"Sorry, girl!" Gina spoke up. "He's with me, Shana baby!"

"Oh really!" Shantae said as she and Boo Man walked up.

Shantae then gave Gina a look that caused the girl to suck her teeth and quickly release her hold on Gabe. She then looked at Gabe a moment and met his eyes before looking at Duke and Melody.

"Y'all just getting here?" Shantae asked.

"We been here a few minutes out front," Duke replied. "You not with ya man Silk? Where he at?"

"He's not my man!" Shantae stated, cutting her eyes to Gabe and seeing him talking with Gina. She then looked back at Duke and said, "His ass left to go out to the truck a few minutes ago for something. He should be back soon!"

"Well, I'ma get back up with y'all. I see they got something to drink," Duke announced. "Gabe, what's up? You rolling with me or Gina?"

"I guess that answers my question!" Duke said laughing as both Melody and an upset Gina followed him through the crowd.

Once Duke and the rest of them left, Shantae looked at Boo Man, who was talking to a few guys who had walked up to him. She motioned that she was going outside.

"Follow me!" she then said to Gabe.

Gabe did as he was told and followed Shantae through the house and out to the back patio. The back yard was just as crowded as the front. But Gabe did get a good look at the shape of Shantae's nice, firm, bubble butter she had inside some tight-fitting blue jeans.

"You looking in the wrong direction, player!" Shantae told him, looking back over her shoulder to catch him staring at her ass.

"I'd rather stare at what has my interest than at what doesn't!" Gabe told her as the two of them stopped next to a mango tree.

"Whatever, nigga!" Shantae stated as she turned to face him. "So what you doing up in here with Gina? You two fucking around already?"

"You asking why?"

"What?"

"What's ya reason for asking?"

"Because I want to know!"

"Why?"

"Nigga, don't play with me!" Shantae told him, stepping up into Gabe's face. "Is you fucking with Gina or not? Answer the fucking question!"

Gabe slowly smirked as he stood staring into Shantae's eyes. He then opened his mouth to reply, just as two females rushed up on them and yelled something about Silk about to get into a fight with somebody named Tank.

Shantae took off at the mention of the name Tank. She pushed past the two females that warned her and busted through the back patio door moments later, rushing to get to the front of the house.

* * *

Shantae saw the crowd form into a huge and wide circle as soon as she flew out the front door. She pushed through the crowd in the front yard and saw seven guys circling around Boo Man and Silk. She burst through the crowd and ran straight up to Tank, who was in Silk's face.

"Muthafucker, you just don't learn, do you? What the fuck you got going on?"

"Bitch, back up outta my face!" Tank told her, but he made the mistake of mussing Shantae in the face.

"Muthafucker!" Shantae yelled.

Within seconds, she had her razor out and pressed it against Tank's throat, only to pause when she felt the familiar touch of a gun pressed against the side of her head.

"Ho, you really must be trying to go see ya

maker!" one of Tank's boys told her as he pressed a 9mm Beretta against the side of her head.

"I wonder who you're about to meet, playboy!" Shantae heard seconds before she heard a bottle explode.

When the gun was instantly snatched away from the side of her head, Shantae spun around to see Gabe with the gun in his hand and pointing it straight at Tank. The guy who had the gun pressed against Shantae's head was now in a chokehold.

"So this how it's gonna go," Gabe calmly stated while maintaining a tight hold on homeboy's neck. He then called to Shantae: "So, what we doing, ma? Am I dropping these niggas or what? It's your decision."

Shantae saw the fear on Tank's face and on the face of the guy who Gabe had in a chokehold.

She shook her head and said, "Let 'em go, Gabe!"

Gabe nodded his head in response to Shantae's request and then said, "I guess ya maker must of been watching over you niggas or y'all got one of them praying grandmothers. I tell you what though. Shantae said you niggas are good to go, but I'ma need y'all to do something before you stupid muthafuckers go! Strip!"

4

G abe stood with Shantae and the others as they all stood watching Tank and his boys run butt-ass naked down the street, after they had them strip naked of their clothes and even their jewels. Gabe stood awaiting the money he had taken from the pockets of the seven niggas Shantae and her people were beefing with, while everybody stood laughing their asses off.

"Yo, Gabe!" Duke called, walking up beside his boy. "Dude, you is wild as fuck! That shit was funny as hell!"

"Where you know I can get rid of these chains?" Gabe asked as he slid the $403 into his pocket.

"You tryin' to sell that shit?" Duke asked. "I may know this white dude that'll give you a good price."

"When can you take me to him?" Gabe asked, just as Shantae and the others walked up on the two of them.

"Goddamn, gun slinger!" Boo Man said jokingly. "That was some wild shit you just pulled!"

"You good?" Gabe asked, looking directly at

Shantae.

"Yeah!" Shantae answered, holding Gabe's eyes. "You've done that before, haven't you?"

"Done what before?" Gabe asked, looking to his left and feeling someone brush up against him, only to see it was Gina.

Shantae mean-mugged Gina, who was blankly ignoring her and continuing to hug up on Gabe. Shantae kept quiet for the moment, deciding to just deal with Gina later. She focused back on Gabe.

"Robbing! You've done it before, haven't you?"

"Naw, ma!"

"Bullshit!" Silk spoke up. "You handled that almost as smooth as I would have!"

"I think the boy's smoother than you, Silk, my nigga!" Boo Man stated, causing the others to laugh.

"Yo, look, y'all!" Duke spoke up this time. "Whether Gabe's handled this type of shit before or not, this isn't the time to talk about this shit!"

Shantae agreed that Duke was right as she turned to say something to Gabe, only to see Gina drag him off back into the crowd.

"You look disappointed."

"What you just say?" Shantae asked, after looking around and seeing Silk.

"You heard me! You look disappointed that Gina got to Superboy before you could!"

"Whatever, Silk, with that shit!" she replied, walking off and leaving Silk where his ass was watching her.

* * *

Gabe was kicking it with Duke, Melody, and Gina, who wouldn't leave his side the rest of the night. Duke introduced Gabe to some new people, and some women slid a few numbers by females who slyly slid pieces of paper with their numbers into his hand or smoothly into his pocket as they passed him.

Duke left the party a little after one in the morning. He first stopped and they all got something to eat at a Denny's. Next, he dropped off Gina, who made Gabe walk her to the front door. She stole a kiss from him, which was a clear message to the boy that she wanted to fuck him.

Duke next dropped off Melody and spent five minutes at the front door with her. He gave her a kiss goodbye, and then he walked back to his Explorer after she stepped inside the house.

"My fault, my nigga!" Duke told Gabe as he

was starting the truck.

"You cool!" Gabe replied as Duke pulled off. "When you wanna get up with me about this guy you know who's willing to get these chains up off me?"

"We can do that tomorrow if you want."

"That'll work!"

"That's what it is then!" Duke stated, before asking Gabe a question. "Real talk, my nigga. You ever get down with robbing a bitch before?"

"Naw!" Gabe answered. "Why?"

"You just seem like you knew what the fuck you was doing when shit was going down. I mean, you handled shit smooth as hell, my nigga!"

"You rob?"

"I do a little something!" Duke said with a smirk.

"That shit be worth it?" Gabe asked him, seeing the look on his face.

"Most of the time. Depends on the niggas you robbing!" Duke told him. "It's really all in the watching and planning shit out, but don't get me wrong though. Sometimes it's moments when you can't plan shit out and you just gotta act. Those are the times where you gotta bang a nigga's ass up no questions, take what the fuck you want, and then get ghost!"

"You ever had to drop a nigga?"

"You mean body someone?"

"Pretty much!"

"Truthfully, my nigga. I've busted a few muthafuckers, but I'm never around to see if a nigga dies behind my shit. Once I get what I'm after, I'm in the wind!"

"What's normally your choice of items?"

"Cash, gold, drugs, and anything worth something that I can get cash for, but it's always the first three I focus on first."

Gabe nodded his head in understanding after listening to Duke. He thought about the feeling he caught after laying down Tank and his boys. He thought about the cash that was now inside his pocket. Gabe felt a smile spread across his lips but then changed the subject.

"Where you get ya sound from you got in this thing? I'ma need some for the Caprice I got off Gina's mom."

"First, you need to fix that muthafucker up!" Duke laughed. "I tell you what I'll do! I've got this homeboy who's a monster on working and hooking cars up. I'ma introduce you to him tomorrow, but I ain't gonna lie to you. I know you say you just move here, but if you plan on fucking with my dude to work on that shit you got at your pop's house, you gonna need some cash and a lot of it!"

"I got it under control, playboy!" Gabe told him, thinking about the decision he made to hold onto the Beretta he took from Tank's homeboy.

Gabe finally made it home and dapped up with Duke. He agreed to hook back up with him early in the afternoon once he got up. Gabe got out of the Explorer, headed to the front door, and dug out the house key that Nicole gave him before he left. Once he walked inside, he heard the TV still on but all the lights were out other than in the kitchen. Gabe locked the front door behind him and then walked over to turn off the TV, only to find Nicole asleep on the sofa under a thick blanket.

Gabe was a little surprised that she was actually waiting up for him. He shut off the TV and, for a moment, sat and watched Nicole sleeping. He then turned and headed upstairs to his bedroom.

Once he walked into his room, he closed and locked the door behind him. He then pulled out everything from his pockets and set them on the fold-out table beside the bed. He then pulled out the Beretta from the front of his jeans before sitting down on the side of the bed. He looked at the gun for a few minutes and thought about the decision he made as well as how shit played out back at the party with the nigga, Tank, and his boys.

"Fuck it! Ain't nobody giving me shit anyway! I'm really on my own out here!"

Gabe made the decision and slid the Beretta under his mattress. He then undressed and climbed into bed. The last thought on his mind before he fell into an easy sleep was of his mother.

5

G abe was awoken by the loud shit-talking that he recognized was coming from his father. He lay where he was for a few minutes just listening to his father's indirect bullshit, which he soon realized was directed at him. He threw the sheet off of his body and then climbed from the bed. Gabe shook this head and continued to listen to his father.

Gabe grabbed what he needed to take a quick shower and left the bedroom. He passed Aaron and accepted the hard brush of the shoulder the boy gave him as they passed each other. He shut the bathroom door behind him and locked it as he then got himself ready for a shower. Eight minutes later, Gabe left the bathroom and was headed back to his room, only to run into Nicole coming up the stairs.

"Gabriel!"

Gabe stopped and turned back toward Nicole. He remembered how she was last night and what she tried to do, and he soon found himself apologizing.

"Nicole! Look, I'm sorry about last night. I didn't expect to be out that late!"

Nicole was surprised by his apology and was at a loss for words for a few moments, before she then got control of herself.

"Look, Gabriel. I understand things are hard for you right now, but I need you to help me out a little. If you're going to stay out late like that, then I want you to at least call my cell phone and let me know you'll be home late. And while I'm talking, I might as well tell you that I'll take you to school on Monday and enroll you. You'll be going to Aaron and Kyle's school, okay?"

"A'ight!" Gabe replied, again catching the surprised look that appeared on her face at how easily he agreed. "I'll get a cell phone while I'm out today. I'm going with the guy from last night to see if I can get the car out front fixed."

Nicole was truly surprised at how open and easy Gabe was now being with her.

"Thank you!" she replied with a smile.

* * *

Gabe was dressed in blue Polo jeans, a white Hanes T-shirt over a white wifebeater, and a pair of Air Max, with a blue leather blazer-style jacket. He was standing outside by his Caprice when Duke pulled up. Gabe explained that he wanted to take care of things with the car first and then they could check out his friend for the chains. He walked back to the Caprice and tossed the backpack he was carrying over onto the passenger seat as he was climbing into the car.

After leaving his father's house and following Duke across town to southwest Miami, Gabe pulled up in front of a garage-like warehouse and saw numerous cars, trucks, and SUVs parked inside the lot. Other cars were either being worked on under the hood or getting painted.

Gabe parked his Caprice and followed Duke into the garage to meet a Spanish man named Hernandez. Gabe then shook his hand as Duke made introductions.

"So, what's up?" Hernandez asked, after meeting Gabe. "What can I do for you fellas?"

Gabe spoke up in perfect and clear Spanish. He broke down everything that he needed and wanted done to the Chevy Caprice convertible.

Hernandez nodded his head and asked, "You Spanish?"

"Dominican," Gabe answered in Spanish.

"Mixed?" Hernandez asked, continuing their conversation in Spanish.

Gabe nodded his head in response.

He then switched back to English and asked,

"So what are you going to charge me?"

"Let's go check out your wheels primo!" Hernandez told him, nodding to Gabe to lead the way.

* * *

"What was all that Spanish shit back there with you and Hernandez?" Duke asked Gabe as they were leaving the auto body and paint shop.

"Just a little background information!" Gabe replied. "I'ma need to get a cell phone too. You cool with that?"

"No pressure, my nigga!" Duke answered, but then remembered something. "Yeah, I almost forgot! Shantae wanted me to give you her number to call her. She wanna holla at you about something."

"What's up with that nigga Silk?" Gabe asked, changing the topic.

"What about 'im?" Duke asked. "Dude's good people!"

"I hear you. I'm talking about with dude and Shantae though."

Duke smiled after understanding what his boy was talking about.

"You feeling Shantae, ain't you?" Duke asked.

"That's not answering my question."

"A'ight! They used to have a thing back when we was younger around like six and seven years old, but we was kids then, my nigga."

"Nothing recent?"

"Naw!" Duke answered. "Shantae's too focused on her paper chase, which is why I'm surprised she wants you to hit her up!"

Gabe nodded his head at the information he had just received and said nothing further. He simply dug out his Newports and offered one to Duke.

* * *

Shantae felt herself getting more and more upset the longer she waited, while supposedly watching the two new victims that she, Boo Man, and Silk were planning to hit up. She looked over at Silk in the passenger seat of his F-150, who was watching her instead of watching their victims.

"What the fuck is wrong with you?" Shantae asked with an attitude. "Fuck is you watching me for?"

"I should be asking your ass what's up with you!" Silk told her. "You been zoned the fuck out since we left the house. Where you at?"

"I'm right here, nigga!"

"That's what ya' mouth say!"

"Fuck is you trying to say?"

"I'm saying that ever since—!"

Shantae and Silk instantly snatched out their hammers when they heard the back door open behind them. They spun around only to freeze after seeing Boo Man.

"What the fuck!" Boo Man said, after seeing the bangers in both Shantae's and Silk's hands. "What the fuck is wrong with you two?"

"Nothing!" Shantae said, turning back around inside her seat. "What you saw, Boo?"

Shantae started up the F-150 and drove off from in front of the apartments that their victims went into. She then drove while listening to Boo Man explain everything to her and Silk. She heard her cell phone finally began to ring, so she dug it out and saw that it was Duke on the other line.

"What, Duke?"

"Where you at?"

"Handling something with Boo Man and Silk. Where the fuck you at?"

"Relax, Shantae. I handled what you asked me to handle. The man's buying a phone now as we speak. I'm just outside waiting on him to finish."

"Where y'all going after y'all leave there?"

"He wanna buy that Malibu the nigga Tony left at his sister's crib. I'ma take him over there and see if she'll sell it to him."

"She owes me a favor. So tell her I said whatever she charges him to take off the $600 she owes me from it."

"Goddamn!"

"Shut the fuck up, Duke!"

"I ain't say shit!"

"You ain't have to. I know your ass, nigga!" she told her brother. "I'ma come by your girl's house later. Be there!"

After hanging up the phone on her brother and dropping the cell phone into her lap, Shantae glanced over to her right and once again caught Silk watching her with his face balled up. But before she could say anything, he looked away and shook his head.

* * *

Gabe left the T-Mobile store after buying a new cell phone, and texted Nicole his new number as he had promised her he would. He had the money on him that he got for the six chains and four gold grills that he took from the nigga Tank and his boys. He then met with the female who Duke was talking to him about who was trying to get rid of a 2005 Chevy Malibu, only to find out that shorty wanted $1,200 for the thing.

"Shantae says you owe her $600," Duke told the girl. "That's true, right?"

"Tell Shantae I ain't forget. I'ma pay her back the money, Duke," the female told him with an attitude.

"Don't even worry about it!" Duke told her with a smile. "She told me to tell you to take off the $600 you owe out of what you were charging my nigga Gabe here."

"What?" she yelled.

Gabe smiled as he counted out $600, which he gave to the female.

"Go ahead and get them keys and paperwork for me, shorty."

Five minutes later after leaving from buying the used Chevy Malibu that drove smoothly and was in better shape than he expected, Gabe turned into the Wendy's behind Duke. He parked beside a Nissan Maxima. He shut off the Malibu and was climbing out, just as his new phone went off inside his pocket. Gabe saw that it was Nicole calling, just as he was about to meet Duke at the entrance to Wendy's.

"What's up, Nicole?"

"Hey, Gabriel. I was just calling to say thank you for sending me your number. Are you okay?"

"Yeah. I'm good. Just about to get something to eat."

"All right. I'll let you go, but call me if you need me."

After hanging up with Nicole, Gabe shook his head and smirked, thinking about how she was beginning to grow on him. He stood with Duke in line until the two of them made it to the counter, where a smiling white girl stood waiting to take their orders.

After ordering their food, they noticed that the girl slid extra food onto their trays. Both Duke and Gabe also caught the piece of paper the girl set down onto Gabe's tray.

"It's like that, huh?" Duke asked, smiling as he and Gabe left the counter together.

"I guess!" Gabe replied as he and Duke sat down at a window table.

"Well, you better be careful!" Duke told him jokingly. "Shantae will snap about her shit; and from what it's looking like, she's claiming yo' ass, bruh!"

Gabe chuckled as he opened the wrapper of

his Double Stack sandwich. He then looked up just in time to catch the box Chevy turning into the Wendy's parking lot. He stared as it drove around into the drive-thru. Gabe looked back at Duke to see his boy watching him.

"You see the Chevy just now?"

Duke smiled as Gabe tossed his car keys over to him across the table before sliding out from his seat. He was right behind Gabe jogging over to the Chevy Malibu.

Gabe broke off from Duke and jogged around the back end of the Wendy's and saw the box Chevy parked at the ordering board. He pulled out his Beretta as he ducked low and crept up to the passenger side of the Chevy. He snatched open the unlocked passenger door, and before the homeboy behind the wheel had time to turn fully around from leaning out the window while ordering, Gabe had his Beretta pressed to the back of homeboy's grapefruit.

"Act up, and I promise I'ma act up in this bitch, nigga! You know what it is, bitch?"

6

S hantae parked outside of Melody's house and already felt herself getting upset since she didn't see Duke's Ford Explorer parked anywhere. She shut off the engine to her 2003 Ford Mustang convertible and was pulling out her cell phone when she saw Melody walking out to her car. She hit the locks to let her inside.

"Hey, Shantae, girl!" Melody said as she climbed into the Mustang. "What you doing way over here?"

"I'm supposed to be meeting Duke and Gabe's ass over here!"

"I just got off the phone with Duke just a few minutes ago," Melody told Shantae, seeing the girl's face ball up in anger. "Shantae, relax, girl! Duke said he was coming by in a little while."

"His ass supposed to be here already, Melody."

"He say he and Gabe got into something and had to drive out to southwest Miami."

"Southwest Miami?"

"That's what Duke say!" Melody told her, just as Shantae started up the Mustang.

"You coming with me or staying here?"

Shantae asked Melody. "I'm about to go find Duke."

"You know where they at?" Melody asked as she shut the car door.

"There's only one place I know Duke could be right now if he's in southwest Miami," she told Melody, speeding off from in front of her girl's house.

Shantae sped faster than she normally drove since getting her Mustang a year ago. She swung the car down the street on which she knew the auto body and paint shop was that Duke's homeboy, Hernandez, worked at. Sure as shit is stank, she saw the Explorer parked inside the gated parking lot. She slowed down the Mustang and turned into the parking lot.

"Girl, there they ass go right there!" Melody said, staring at both Duke and Gabe smoking and talking with some other guys at the garage.

"Come on!" Shantae told Melody as she was parking right beside an Escalade truck.

Both girls got out of the car and started toward Duke and Gabe.

* * *

"You see this?" Duke asked Gabe after nudging him.

"Yeah! I see it!" Gabe answered while staring

at Shantae as she headed straight for him, staring angrily at him.

He slowly smirked as he admitted to himself that the girl was sexy as hell with her tomboyish yet still feminine ways.

"You think I'm something to play with, don't you, nigga!" Shantae asked as soon as she stopped in front of Gabe. "I know Duke told you what the fuck I said."

"Yeah! He told me!" Gabe replied, but then asked, "What you doing out here, Shan?"

"What?"

"You heard me, ma! Answer the question!"

"Nigga! I came to—!"

"Naw!" Gabe interrupted her. "In the streets I'ma give you the respect the clowns out here will also give you, and I expect you to hold me down the same way. So we gonna try this again. What you doing here?"

Shantae stared at Gabe and saw both Duke and Melody were watching her with smirks on their lips. Shantae quickly grabbed Gabe's arm when he started to walk off.

"All right, nigga! Damn, boy!"

"I'm listening!" Gabe answered.

"I wanted to find out why you still haven't called me yet!" she admitted. "I know Duke told you what I said, so why hasn't yo' ass—I mean, why didn't you call me?"

Gabe nodded his head after hearing what Shantae had to say.

"I'm not in the habit of explaining myself, but for you I'll explain. Just not right now!" Gabe told her.

"What?" Shantae yelled as Gabe began walking off with Duke right behind him.

Shantae looked at Melody, who shrugged her shoulders in indication that she didn't know what was going on.

Shantae looked back in the direction where Duke and Gabe had walked. She started to go off when she saw a charcoal-gray Chevy Malibu with midnight-black tinted windows, 22-inch Forgiato Magro-L wheels, and some Nexen tires. She saw Duke's homeboy, Hernandez, climb from the car once it stopped directly in front of where Gabe and Duke were standing.

Shantae watched Gabe talking with Hernandez, and then saw the nice-sized knot of money he pulled out from his pocket. He handed a few bills to Hernandez, only to receive the keys to the Malibu in return. Shantae then walked over to Gabe and Duke, with Melody right alongside her.

"Ummm! Do somebody wanna tell me where this car came from?"

"It's the one Vic left at his sister's house before he got sent up the road!" Duke told Shantae as Gabe walked around to the driver's side and climbed into the Malibu.

"You mean that's how that shit looked before Vic went in?" Shantae asked as Gabe started the Malibu back up.

"Naw!" Duke answered as he dropped his arm around Melody's shoulders. "We just had the rims put on and also—!"

Duke never got the chance to finish what he was saying, when Kanye West's "Can't Tell Me Nothing" banged from the Malibu's sound system. Duke broke out in a smile, staring at his boy as the passenger window slowly slid down.

Shantae saw Gabe motion her over to the car, so she walked over to the passenger side window.

"Get in!" Gabe yelled over the music, smiling as Shantae tossed her car keys to Duke and then climbed inside the Malibu.

Gabe hit the car horn as he pulled off and left the shop's parking lot.

* * *

Gabe rode around a little while after leaving the auto body and paint shop. He then pulled into a Miami Subs shop a short while later, since he never got a chance to eat back at Wendy's. He parked the Chevy Malibu, and then he and Shantae got out and headed inside the restaurant. They fell in line behind five people waiting to order. Shantae froze up when she felt Gabe's body press up against hers from the back and his right hand slide around her waist to rest on her stomach.

"Relax, ma!" he whispered into her ear. "I don't bite, you know!"

Shantae was unable to really relax with him being so close. Gabe immediately sensed it because he moved his hand and stepped back away from her. She felt instantly upset and turned her head to look back at him, only to see him looking elsewhere. She followed the direction he was looking and saw two bitches smiling and staring back at him.

"So, you gonna just disrespect me like that, nigga?" she asked, punching Gabe in his mid-section that was surprisingly hard.

Gabe turned his head, looked back at Shantae, and met her eyes.

"How exactly is my looking disrespecting you, Shan?"

"Because you supposed to be with one nigga!

Don't get them hos hurt!"

"With you, huh?"

"That's what the fuck I said!"

"Really?" Gabe said as he reached out, grabbed Shantae around the small of her waist, and pulled her up against him.

He slid his hand down and gently gripped her ass, all the while feeling how stiff her body was again.

"So you with me and act like this? You supposed to be mine, so why the fuck is you so nervous?"

Shantae stumbled after Gabe suddenly released her and stepped around her. She spun around to see him walk up to the counter as the last customer left with their food.

* * *

There was little talking while the two ate their sub sandwiches. Shantae rode back to Melody's house with Gabe, trying to find something to say yet coming up with nothing.

Once they arrived back at Melody's house, they saw her sitting on Duke's lap with Gina standing beside them on the porch. When Shantae saw Gina's face break out in a huge smile, she turned around to see Gabe just climbing out of his car.

"Gabe!" Shantae yelled as she jumped out of the Malibu and spun back to face Gabe across the top of the car.

"I'm telling you now! Do not play with me! Keep that bitch out of your face, or I promise I will whoop her ass!"

Gabe heard Shantae but didn't bother to say a thing. He shut the car door and then walked around the car, just as Gina came walking over to meet him.

"Hey, baby daddy!" Gina cried happily as she threw her arms up around Gabe's neck to hug him.

Gina never saw Shantae rushing toward her, but she screamed when Gabe swung her away hard and caught a punch to the mouth from Shantae.

"Oh my God!" Gabe heard Gina say behind him as both Melody and Duke rushed over to them.

Gabe stood staring straight at Shantae and finally spoke up: "You feel better now?"

"Gabe, I am not playing with you, nigga! You either gonna respect me and keep these hos out your face, or I will beat every last one I see up in your face! Try me!"

"Shantae!"

"Shut up, Duke!" Shantae yelled. "This between me and my man! His ass thinks I'm playing with him!"

When Shantae looked back at Gabe and saw him smirking at her with a bloody lip, she went off.

"Muthafucker, quick fucking smiling at me! I'm not fucking playing with you!"

"Come here, ma!" Gabe calmly told her, still smirking.

"Fuck you!" Shantae told him.

"Come here, ma!" Gabe repeated, reaching out for her, only for Shantae to snatch away.

"Don't touch me!" she told Gabe, even as he grabbed her around the waist and pulled her up against him.

Shantae pushed against his chest, but not hard enough to really get away.

"Stop, ma!" Gabe told her, feeling Shantae slowly stop fighting him. He licked the blood from his lip and then said, "So, now you mad at me, ma?"

"Gabe, don't play with me, boy! You know what I told you!"

"A'ight! You got that!"

"Got what?"

"I'ma keep 'em out my face, but you gotta

trust me a little and relax, Shan!"

Shantae sucked her teeth and rolled her eyes, but found herself wrapping her arms around Gabe and laying her head onto his chest.

"I never thought I'd see this day! Shantae actually got a boyfriend that can deal with her!" Melody said.

"I'ma pray for my nigga's safety!" Duke said jokingly, causing the others to bust out laughing.

G abe was up early the next morning watching ESPN in the den. By the time Nicole made it downstairs dressed in a gray pantsuit, that actually looked good on her and gave her a business yet sexy type of look, Gabe shut off the TV and left the den to meet her in the kitchen.

"You want breakfast before we leave, Gabriel?" Nicole asked as she walked past him.

"Nicole!" Gabe called out, getting her attention and catching her at the entrance to the kitchen. "I want to, ummmm, take you out to breakfast!"

Nicole nodded in agreement and said, "At least let me put on the coffee for your father!"

"I'll wait outside," Gabe told her as he backed away, turned, and headed toward the front door.

Gabe waited outside, and in less than five minutes Nicole walked out the door with his father on her trail complaining about something. Gabe really couldn't hear their conversation. Gabe did catch the look his father shot him, but he ignored it as Nicole walked over to her car where he stood waiting.

"Before we go for breakfast, I need to get some gas, okay?" Nicole announced as she was unlocking her car door with her key remote.

"I'll follow behind you," Gabe replied as he headed out to his car that was parked in front of the house.

Once Gabe sat inside the Malibu, he tossed his backpack onto the passenger seat and started up the engine. He waited until Nicole backed out of the driveway and pulled off. He then pulled off behind her, all the while aware of his father angrily staring at him as he drove off.

They made a stop at the gas station, where Gabe pumped and paid for the gas for both of them. They then drove over to Granny B's Soul Food Kitchen, where they were seated and ordered breakfast, and Gabriel asked for the bill.

"Gabriel, can I ask you something?" Nicole inquired a short while after they were seated and had begun eating.

"What's up, Nicole?" Gabe replied, lifting his eyes from his plate to look across the table at her.

"What happened?" she asked him. "You were once so quiet and wouldn't actually talk to me, but now you're suddenly different toward me. Why?"

Gabe continued to eat and remained quiet for a few moments. He then swallowed his food and spoke up.

"Truthfully, you reminded me of my mom the night I got home late and you were asleep in the front room after trying to wait up for me. She used to do that some nights I came in late."

"Oh!" Nicole got out, unsure of exactly what to say after hearing Gabe's confession. She changed the subject and then asked, "Will you tell me how it is that you're able to spend all of this money? One moment I see you with an old beat-up car, and then the next I see you with the Chevy Malibu that you're driving now. How?"

"A friend of mine introduced me to a new job. I get paid by the work I do."

"Labor work?"

He nodded his head yes.

"Well, I'm happy you found a job then!" she told him proudly. "At least you're not lazy like both of my sons are!"

Gabe cracked a smile at what Nicole had just told him.

"Thanks, Nicole!" he replied after a moment.

Nicole smiled across the table at Gabe after hearing his thanks. She then reached across the table and took his hand. She smiled even wider when he gently gripped her hand.

"You're always welcome, Gabriel. I promise, sweetheart!"

* * *

They finally made it out to the new senior high school where Gabe allowed Nicole to enroll him. He then accepted the kiss to the cheek she gave him before she said goodbye and then turned and left him inside the school standing at the front entrance. He watched her until her car disappeared up the street. Gabe then turned and walked back into the school, pulling out his cell phone and pulling up Duke's number. He hit the send button and called his boy.

"What up?"

"This Gabe!"

"Where the fuck you at, nigga? We waiting for your ass now!"

"I'm at the main office. Nicole just left the school after enrolling me."

"A'ight! Come to the back of the school where the student parking lot is. You'll see us posted by the nigga Silk's truck. You driving?"

"Yeah!"

"Drive 'round back. I was telling both Boo

Man and Silk about the ride."

"Yeah, a'ight! Where's Shan at?"

"Staring at me! You wanna talk to her?"

"Naw!"

"You know she's gonna be heated since you ain't call her or ask to speak to her!"

"I know!" Gabe replied, smiling as he walked out the front entrance of the school. "I'ma be around back in a few minutes, playboy!"

* * *

After hanging up with Gabe, Duke looked up and wasn't surprised to see a heated-looking Shantae walking straight over to him. He slid his phone back into his pocket just as his sister stopped in front of him.

"That was Gabe, wasn't it?" Shantae asked him, with arms folded across her chest.

"Yeah!" Duke answered still smiling.

"Why the hell didn't you let me talk to him, Duke?"

"He didn't ask!"

"Nigga, I wouldn't give a fuck if—!"

"There he go now!" Duke announced, cutting off Shantae from her ranting and raving.

Shantae turned around to see where her so-called boyfriend was, who at the moment was in trouble with her. She stared at Gabe's Chevy Malibu as it turned into the school parking lot and slowed down the lot, coming to a stop in front of her and Duke. As she watched the driver's side window slide down, she balled up her face when she saw a smirking Gabe staring at her.

"What's up, ma?" Gabe called out, still smirking at her. "Come here real quick."

"Fuck you, Gabe!" Shantae told him, turning and walking back over to where Silk and Boo Man were standing.

Gabe chuckled as he sat watching Shantae. He then looked over at Duke as his boy walked up to his car door. He dapped up with Duke.

"What's up, playboy?"

"What up, my nigga?" Duke replied with a smile. "I told you she was gonna be heated."

"Naw!" Gabe stated, looking over at Shantae and catching her watching him.

She looked away once they locked eyes.

"She just wants some attention right now. I got her though!"

"You two a trip!" Duke said, shaking his head. He then bent down and leaned on the car's window sill. "You trying to put in some work?"

"Talk to me!" Gabe told him, getting serious

at the mention of putting in work.

Gabe listened to Duke explain about the new hit he had set up. He learned about some hustler who went by the name of Gator. Gabe found out that it was around the time the so-called hustler was supposedly picking up his trap money from the four traps he was running and owned.

"What do the dude's numbers look like?" Gabe asked once Duke finished talking.

"Shit! From what I've been seeing, two of that nigga's spots are pulling in a little over twenty-some stacks a week. But his other two are bringing in a little less, but not by much," Duke broke down to Gabe.

"So, about the spot we running down on this nigga?" Gabe started asking, before Duke spoke up.

"We hitting his ass at the spot out in Wynwood. That's where he does his last pickup and drop-off, so when we catch his ass, he gonna have all three pickups along with the cash in Wynwood."

Gabe nodded his head in agreement to what Duke was telling him. He did some quick counting in his head and smiled at the split he and Duke were going to make.

"What time we leaving?"

"In twenty minutes!" Duke replied, just as a pissed-off Shantae walked over.

"Ummm, excuse fucking me!" she interrupted. "Duke, Melody just pulled up with Gina and Lisa. Them and I need to talk to Gabe's ass!"

"Twenty minutes, my nigga!" Duke repeated, touching fists with Gabe.

Duke walked off leaving Shantae alone with Gabe, and she wasted no time getting on his ass.

"So, you was just going to sit here and ignore me, right? Yo' ass knew I wanted to talk to you. And first you don't call me and then you just sit here acting like you don't know I'm heated with you. Keep playing, Gabe!"

"You done?"

"What, nigga?"

"If you finish, I wanna kiss!"

"Fuck you!"

Through the open car window, Gabe grabbed Shantae's arm before she could walk off again. He opened the car door with is right hand while maintaining his hold on Shantae's arm with his left. He climbed from the car and switched his hold on her arm, only to pull her up against him.

Within moments, she had her arms wrapped around his neck returning his kiss.

* * *

"Oh my God!" Lisa cried in both shock and disbelief as she stood staring at Shantae, who was not only hugged up with Duke's friend, Gabe, but was tonguing the boy the hell down. "What is going on with them two?"

Melody turned to see what Lisa was talking about, and smiled seeing Shantae and Gabe kissing.

"Yeah! Y'all don't know yet, but Shantae finally got herself a boyfriend, and Gabe got her ass wide open too!"

"Girl, I see it!" Lisa said with a smile as she looked over at Gina. "Gina, girl! I thought you were after Mr. Sexy over there! What happened?"

"Shantae took something!" Boo Man stated, causing everybody but Gina to laugh.

"Dawg, you called that shit straight out! She fought for my nigga Gabe for real!" Duke added.

Melody laughed along with all the others. But she noticed that Gina wasn't laughing at all, nor was Silk, who had an angry expression on his face as he stared straight at both Shantae and Gabe.

* * *

66

Gabe met up with Duke after the first bell rang, never making it to his first-period class. He was now out in the student parking lot again and was climbing inside the passenger seat of Duke's Explorer. Gabe sat quietly as Duke drove off from the school. He checked his banger and made sure everything was okay, and then he pulled out his Newports. He fired one up and chilled back while Duke took them where they were headed.

Ten minutes later, Duke pulled up beside a dark blue Honda Accord that was parked inside an open parking lot off of 27th Avenue. He and Gabe then got out of the SUV and got into the Honda.

"Check the glove compartment," Duke told Gabe as he was starting up the engine.

Gabe found two black ski masks inside the glove compartment box. He tossed one over to Duke and then slid his own onto his head. After getting it into position correctly over his face, he then rolled it upward, leaving it sitting atop his head.

Duke made it out into Wynwood a short while later. He drove past the trap house and pointed out Gator's Aston Martin parted out in front, along with a green Impala SS and a Navigator. Duke then parked three houses down and across the street, and then turned and looked over at Gabe.

"What's up, my nigga? You ready?"

Gabe smirked at Duke and then pulled down his ski mask into place. He climbed from the SUV as Duke was putting on his own mask.

Duke caught up with Gabe and noticed how his boy motioned him to the front. He then saw Gabe jog around to the back of the house. Duke quickly decided that he would trust his boy as he was sliding into the front yard and was creeping up onto the front porch, when the door swung open.

"Oh shit!" the guy stepping out of the front door yelled, after seeing the masked robber.

He threw up his hands and dropped the cell phone he had up to his ear, only to get shoved backward into the house and see his cell phone get smashed under the boots the robber was wearing.

"Where the fuck the—?"

Boom! Boom! Boom!

Duke ducked after the first shot was fired. He then grabbed homeboy at the front door and used him as a shield. Duke then let the .45 he was holding speak out.

Boom! Boom! Boom! Boom!

Duke saw three more dudes with bangers in their hands appear from a side room. He then saw Gator himself. Duke slammed into the closed door he stood in front of with the man he was using as a shield, which turned out to be a bathroom.

"You might as well come the fuck out, muthafucker!" Gator yelled out. "You a dead muthafucker either way, nigga!"

"Shit!" Duke said under his breath as shit got quiet out in the front room.

He sat inside the bathroom wondering where the fuck Gabe was at.

"Playboy, you good? Come on out!" a voice called out from the other side of the door.

After Duke recognized the voice, he pushed the dude he was using as a shield out of the bathroom first. After no shots were fired, Duke looked out and almost burst out laughing when he saw Gator and all his boys all on their knees with their hands behind their heads and finger-laced.

"This muthafucker!"

8

Melody, Boo Man, Silk, Gina, Lisa, Kiki, and Shantae were all waiting outside the student parking lot during lunch break after the school bell went off. Shantae then looked around for Duke and Gabe, since they were the only ones missing. She looked at Melody, and was just about to ask her if she knew where they were, when Silk walked up on her.

"You looking for pretty boy?"

Shantae stared down Silk with a questioning look on her face.

"What did you say?" she faced him directly and asked.

"You heard what the fuck I said!" Silk answered. "You looking for that punk-ass nigga I hear you fucking with now, huh?"

"Who you talking about? Gabe?"

"Who the fuck else?"

"All right! First off, you need to relax how the fuck you talk to me!" Shantae told him. "What the fuck's wrong with you?"

"You just met this nigga, and now you all over this muthafucker!"

"And?"

"And my ass, Shantae! You don't even know this soft-ass dude, and you already all over his ass!"

"Hold up! Nigga, you jealous?" Shantae asked, just as Boo Man called the both of them and announced that Duke and Gabe were pulling up.

Shantae spun around to see Duke's truck pulling into the parking lot.

"Where the hell you two been at?" she called out as Duke pulled to a stop in front of them and Gabe got out of the Explorer and walked around the front.

She forgot all about Silk and walked over to her man. She then wrapped her arms around his waist as he laid his arm around her shoulders.

"We had something to handle!" Duke told his sister as Melody walked over to him.

"Yo!" Boo Man spoke up. "Since everybody's here now, can we please get something to eat? I'm hungry as fuck!"

"You always hungry, nigga!" Duke stated, shaking his head and smiling.

"I'm with Boo Man!" Melody added. "I'm ready to eat too."

Duke agreed to go to Pizza Hut along with

Melody, Gina, and Lisa in his Explorer, while Shantae, Kiki, and Boo Man road with Gabe inside his Malibu. Silk drove solo inside his F-150, but trailed behind the Malibu.

"Goddamn!" Lisa said, spinning around in her seat after hearing and even feeling the bass coming from Gabe's Malibu. She stared through the back window at the car. "What the fuck does that boy got in that shit?"

"A lot!" Duke said with a smile as he turned on his own system, and old-school 2 Pac's "All Eyes on Me" bumped from the Explorer.

* * *

Gabe got through the lunch break and then finished up the second half of school. He half paid attention to what went on in his fifth and six period classes, but when the bell rang, he was out of his seat and one of the top five students who hit the door leaving class. He made it out to the back gate that led into the student parking lot, when he ran into Silk coming out of the gym room.

"My fault, playboy!" Gabe apologized, only for Silk to brush him off and continue walking out the gate.

Gabe shook his head and paid no attention to Silk and his attitude. He then walked out the gate, only to hear his name. Upon looking back, he saw Shantae and Kiki.

"What up, ma?" Gabe asked, dropping his arm around her and nodding to Kiki.

"What you about to do?" Shantae asked as they walked out into the parking lot.

"I gotta handle something with Duke, but then I was coming to chill at the house," Gabe explained. "What you about to do though?"

"I gotta handle something with Boo Man and them, but I'll be home later! You still coming over?"

"Yeah!" Gabe answered as they walked up on Duke with Boo Man, Melody, and Silk. "What's up Duke? You ready?"

"Waiting on you, my nigga!" Duke told him, before turning around and giving Melody a kiss. "We taking your ride?"

"That'll work," Gabe said as he kissed Shantae a little longer than he intended to, since she had her fist balled up on his front before releasing him.

"Make sure you make your way to the house," Shantae added.

Gabe smirked as he gave her ass a squeeze before walking around to the driver's door to his

Malibu. He hit the locks, and then both he and Duke climbed inside the car.

* * *

Shantae watched as Gabe drove off from the school parking lot. She then looked over to her left at Silk.

"If you finished with the other shit, you ready to get this money or what?" Silk questioned her.

"Nigga, is you ready?" Shantae asked, brushing past Silk and walking around to the passenger side of his F-150.

Once they were inside the truck and Silk had pulled away from the parking space, Shantae took the ski mask and her .40 caliber from Boo Man in the back seat. She then pulled off the shirt she was wearing, dug out the black Hanes T-shirt from her backpack, and slipped it on over her sports bra.

They all got themselves together as they drove across town to Brown Subs to the apartment at which that they knew was the spot their two victims hid their dope and money. One of the victims was dating the female to whose apartment it belonged.

"Here we go!" Silk announced as he turned down the street and pulled up in front of the apartment.

He stopped and let Shantae out, and then he drove up to the corner and turned around.

Shantae crossed the street and walked up to the front door of the apartment. She knocked loudly and yelled out one of her victim's names as if she was angrily demanding that he bring his ass outside. She could hear the female inside going off.

Shantae snatched her ski mask into place over her face and glanced around, just as she heard the door knob turn. She swung up her. 40 caliber as the door swung open and caught the female off guard.

"Bitch, you scream and I'ma paint your thoughts all over the front of this apartment!" Shantae warned.

Boo Man and Silk slid up and pushed the female back into the apartment. Shantae followed, and then closed and locked the door behind her.

* * *

Gabe split up the money from the hit on Gator as well as the money they got back from the coke and weed. He kept half a pound of the weed for themselves to smoke. He then packed his share into his backpack while Duke packed his into a

Nike gym bag. Duke led the way through the one-bedroom apartment that he kept as a stash house that nobody knew about until now. He and Gabe then stepped outside.

"You coming back to the crib?" Duke asked as he was locking up the apartment.

"Yeah!" Gabe answered, just as his phone went off from inside his pocket. "Hit up ya sister for me real quick. And see if she's at the house."

Gabe saw on his iPhone that his boy Hernandez was calling.

"What's good, Hernandez?"

Gabe climbed into his car but paused with the door still open as he listened to what Hernandez was telling him. Gabe calmly told his boy that he was on his way, and then he hung up the phone.

"Bruh, what's up?" Duke asked, after seeing the look on Gabe's face.

"That was yo' boy Hernandez. We headed over to the shop now."

"What for?"

"Yo' boy say the shop was hit! My shit's gone!" Gabe answered as he pulled away from Duke's apartment and sighed.

* * *

When Shantae, Boo Man, and Silk were in her

bedroom back at her house, she sat with them and counted the money they found at the stash house. Boo Man split the six bricks of coke while smoking a blunt from the quarter pound of Purple Haze they also found in the apartment.

Shantae dug out her cell phone when it began to ring, and she saw that her brother was on the other line.

"What, Duke?" she answered as she got back to her count.

"Yo! Gabe told me to tell you he's still coming. We about to handle something right now though."

"What's up?"

"It's nothing. We got it!"

"That ain't what I asked you, Duke! Matter of fact, put Gabe on the phone!"

Shantae heard the phone being passed, and Gabe came over the phone a few moments later.

"Yeah!"

"Babe, what's up? What's Duke talking about y'all about to handle something?" Shantae asked.

Shantae listened to her man tell her what had supposedly happened. She jumped off the bed and snatched up her keys and .40 caliber, since she didn't like what she was hearing.

"Gabe, I'm on my way!" she told him, hanging up the phone.

"Where the fuck is you going?" Silk asked, before Shantae could shoot out of her bedroom.

"My man's got a problem. Y'all coming or what?" Shantae asked, leaving the bedroom before either Silk or Boo Man could answer her question.

* * *

Gabe pulled up to the auto body and paint shop, turned his Malibu into the parking area, and saw Hernandez rush out of the garage as soon as he saw Gabe pull up. Gabe parked his Malibu, and both he and Duke got out of the car as Hernandez walked up to them.

"Yo, Gabe! Man, I'm sorry—!"

"Relax!" Gabe said, cutting off Hernandez in a calm voice. "Now, how about you tell me what happened again."

Gabe listened as Hernandez went through the whole story about how the three workers in the shop that day had left on their lunch break. When they returned, the shop had been broken into and his car was missing. Gabe looked at Duke and saw the expression on his boy's face, but said nothing to him. Instead, he turned back around to

Hernandez.

"So, how many rides were taken along with mine?"

"Yours and one more. A blue '73 Caprice drop-top!" Hernandez told him.

Gabe nodded his head and then looked to his right when he heard the engine of Shantae's Mustang flying up the street and stopping in front of the shop.

"Go talk to her. Tell her I said to chill!" Gabe said to Duke.

After Duke walked off, Gabe focused back on Hernandez.

"So you got any ideas who robbed ya spot?"

"I'm clueless!" Hernandez said while shaking his head.

"Gabe!" Shantae called as she, Boo Man, Silk, and Duke walked over to him. "Babe, you okay?"

"I'm good, ma!" Gabe told her, dropping his arm around her shoulders. He then looked back at Hernandez and said, "This is what I want you to do, Hernandez. Get at me as soon as you hear or find out anything about my shit. You got me?"

"You've got my word!" Hernandez promised as Gabe and his friends turned and walked away.

Gabe walked over to Shantae's Mustang and leaned back against the passenger door as Shantae stopped directly in front of him.

"Gabe, what's up?" Duke spoke up first. "You plotting something, my nigga? I know you don't believe that bullshit Hernandez just told you!"

"Naw! I don't!" Gabe said while smirking as he dug out his Newports and pulled out his last one.

He fired up the cigarette, and after taking a pull, he blew the smoke upward into the air.

"Tell me something. Does anybody see anything odd about the area or even about the garage?"

"What you mean?" Duke asked.

"I see all four garages being used," Boo Man spoke up.

"That's one!" Gabe began. "I'll give you guys the answer! He said that two rides were taken, and yet all four garages got a ride in them. Then he said it was robbed—the shop, I mean. But where are the cops? It doesn't even look like the police have been in the area."

"So what are you saying, Gabe?" Shantae asked him.

"Hernandez got the ride!" Boo Man answered, seeing Gabe nodding his head in agreement.

"So what you are planning, Gabe?" Shantae asked, repeating Duke's original question.

"We'll talk later!" Gabe said, with a slow smirk appearing on a face.

9

Two weeks after receiving the call about his car getting stolen from Hernandez's shop, Gabe fell back off the twenty-five-year-old Cuban and went about handling his own business. He was putting away the cash he was making since he planned to move out of his father's house as soon as he possibly could. He began changing his style of robbing by switching from dope boys to robbing jewelry stores. He hit up his first store in North Miami Beach and came away with a duffel bag full of gold, platinum, and even a few gold chains with diamonds in them. He went to see the guy who Duke had introduced him to, who bought the jewelry he had taken when he hit up Tank and his boys. But that jeweler introduced him to another jeweler who was located in Miromar Lakes.

Gabe met Paul Lewis and spent a little over forty-five minutes with the red-headed, white jeweler. He was offered a little over $100,000, which took Paul about twenty minutes to get together for him.

Once Gabe returned to Miami, he paid Duke's friend $15,000 for his help and then drove to his new one-bedroom apartment that he was leasing out in Hollywood. He stole the idea from Duke, and only used the apartment for hiding his money. He put away the money he just hit for and was walking out when his cell phone went off from inside his pocket.

Gabe dug out his iPhone while locking up, and saw that Shantae was calling him.

"What's up, ma?"

Gabe received no response, but he heard what sounded like yelling in the background of the phone. He tried to understand what was being said. He put the phone on speaker and turned the volume all the way up. He then realized it was Shantae and the nigga Silk arguing with each other.

Gabe continued walking to the apartment complex parking lot. He continued to listen to the yelling, but paused at his driver's door when he heard Silk yell out that he loved Shantae. He waited for her to respond to him, which he felt took longer than it should have, followed by Shantae telling Silk to leave.

Gabe shook his head and then hung up the phone and climbed into his Malibu. As he started the car, his phone began to ring again. He expected it to be Shantae calling him right back, only to see that it was Duke.

"What up, playboy?" Gabe answered as he was backing out of his parking space and starting toward the front gate.

"Where you at, my nigga?"

"Rolling! What's up though?"

"I'm headed to the house. You can meet me there. I wanna holla at you about some business."

"Gimme like twenty. Shit!" Gabe screamed as he slammed on the brakes.

He was just about to pull out into the intersection, when he stopped at the sight of a dog that ran out in front of him. He then shot forward from the impact of being hit from the back by another car.

"Muthafucker!"

Gabe shoved open his car door and climbed out, only to hear a female yelling and a dog barking. He shook his head and tried to shake the daze he was feeling.

"Oh my God! Are you okay?" Gabe heard a voice, just before his legs gave out and everything went black.

* * *

Erica couldn't believe she was actually sitting

inside the waiting room of a hospital waiting to find out the condition of a total stranger. But she couldn't help wonder if, at that very moment, the puppy sitting inside her car was messing it up by shitting and pissing everywhere.

"Erica!"

Erica swung her head around to see her friends, one of whom was her roommate, rush into the waiting room. Erica stood up just as her girls hugged her.

"Are you alright?" Ebony asked her roommate and best friend while looking her over from head to toe.

"What the hell happened?" Brittany asked her.

"It was an accident!" Erica said, just as the doctor reappeared in the waiting room.

She then broke away from her friends and walked over to him.

"How is he, Doctor?"

"He has a mild concussion from the bang he took to the head; and other than the busted lip and nose, he should be fine," the doctor informed Erica. "He's relaxing and should be asleep in a little while. Would you like to see him before he goes to sleep?"

"Please!" Erica said as she followed behind the doctor, leaving both Brittany and Ebony in the waiting room.

Erica stopped in front of Room 107 and then followed the doctor inside. She looked past the doctor to see the guy she only knew as Gabriel Green. She met his shockingly gorgeous hazel-green eyes when she walked up beside his bed.

"Hi!"

"I'll leave you two alone!" the doctor announced before leaving the room.

"You remember me, right?" she said as she looked back at him and met his eyes.

"Pretty much!" Gabe said, speaking his first words since waking up. "How did I get here?"

"I called the paramedic after you fell out!" Erica told him as she gently rubbed her hand over his surprisingly soft and curvy black hair. "How do you feel?"

"Like I got hit in the back by a Lexus!" he answered sarcastically.

After seeing the look she gave him with her cat-like, light hazel-brown eyes, he heard himself apologize: "I'm sorry. That wasn't necessary. How you doing?"

"I'm fine!" she answered. "I'm really sorry

about this whole mess, but I was just—oh, never mind!"

"Naw!" Gabe said, holding up his hand. "Go ahead and talk. It's easy to see that something's bothering you, and since I'ma be in this bed until tomorrow, I've got time!"

"You really don't wanna hear about my problems, Gabriel."

"Call me Gabe," he told her. "I wanna know what's up with you since we may now end up being best friends."

Erica smiled down at Gabe and soon found herself seated beside him on his hospital bed. She was telling him about her problems, specifically about walking into her boyfriend's apartment and catching him in the act of sexing another woman who was supposedly his cousin from out of town.

"So that's where you was rushing from when we met?" Gabe asked her once she was finished talking.

Erica nodded her head in response to his question and then remembered the puppy.

"I almost forgot. Your puppy is down inside my car."

"Puppy?"

"The terrier!" she told him. "She was going

crazy after you blacked out, so I took her with me since you had to ride with the EMT."

Gabe simply nodded after listening to her, and then realized he didn't even know her name.

"I see you know my name. So you gonna tell me yours?"

"It's Erica!" she replied with a smile. "Erica Scott!"

* * *

After leaving Gabe's hospital room once he had fallen asleep, after trying to fight it most of the time they were together, Erica went back out to the waiting room to get her friends. The three of them then rode the elevator down to the ground floor. Erica told her friends about Gabriel and said that he was Black and Dominican. But for some unknown reason, she lied about his age to her friends and said he was nineteen, even though he was actually turning eighteen in three weeks.

Erica walked through the parking lot and toward her busted-front Lexus. She said goodbye to Brittany, and then she and her roommate, Ebony, continued walking to her car.

"Erica, whose dog?" Ebony asked as soon as she stepped to the passenger-side window and the tan puppy began barking at her from inside the car.

"She's Gabe's!"

"Who?"

"Gabriel, Ebony!" Erica corrected.

She smiled to herself as she unlocked the car doors and then climbed inside, only to have the puppy jump into her lap.

"Hey, cutie!"

"Are you planning on keeping that dog?" Ebony asked.

"Just until Gabriel gets out of the hospital tomorrow," Erica answered as she started the car, surprised that it did, in fact, start.

She backed out of the parking space.

"You mind if we stop and get her some food to eat?"

"Who? The dog, Erica?" Ebony asked.

"Yeah!" Erica replied as she glanced down at the puppy lying in her lap. "She has to eat too, Ebony."

* * *

Shantae tried Gabe's cell number for the tenth time, and once again was sent straight to his voice message. She was pissed off as well as worried. But she was more worried than actually upset after she realized their phones had been connected for about twelve minutes during the time she and Silk were arguing about her relationship with Gabe. She was still surprised hearing that Silk had confessed that he was in love with her and had always been—even from back when they were kids with their crush they had on each other.

Shantae shook her thoughts away. She tried calling Gabe's phone number again, but just as before she got his voice message.

"Gabe, please! Answer the phone, babe!"

10

G abe was finally being released from the hospital after the car accident the day before. He was surprised when Erica walked into his hospital room, just as he was putting on his shoes.

"Hey, you!" Erica said to Gabe with a smile. "How you feeling?"

"A little sore, but good!" Gabe told her, pushing up from the hospital bed. "What are you doing here?"

"Picking you up!" she replied. "You ready to go?"

"Definitely!"

Erica and Gabe left the hospital room, stopped by the nurse desk to sign out, and then took the elevator down to the ground floor.

"I've got someone inside the car waiting for you!" she told Gabe as they stepped off the elevator.

Gabe followed Erica from the hospital and walked out to a drop-top Jaguar XK. He smiled when he heard the barking puppy from yesterday. He opened the passenger door and picked up the terrier before he sat down in the seat.

"She misses you!" Erica said, smiling at the sight of the puppy getting playful with Gabe. "Where we going?"

"Your place!" Gabe replied as he picked up the puppy and looked her over.

Erica looked over at Gabe at his request to go to her place. She didn't understand why she didn't question him; instead, she found herself heading in the direction of her and Ebony's condominium.

Erica dug out her cell phone after hearing it ring. She saw that her sister was on the other line.

"Hello!"

She listened to her sister explain that she was on her way to her place and needed her to hold something for her. Erica agreed and then hung up the phone.

"What happened to the Lexus?"

Erica looked over at Gabe as he sat stroking the puppy's back as she chewed on his finger.

"I had it picked up and taken to a shop to get it fixed. This is a rental," she informed him.

"Where's my ride?"

"It was towed away after the accident. I have the information where it's at back at the apartment."

Gabe nodded his head and laid his head back and shut his eyes. Erica drove them to her place, giving him time to think about a few things.

* * *

"Gabe!" Erica said, gently nudging him to wake him from his sleep.

The puppy also woke up at the same time with a yawn.

Gabe lifted his head from the head rest and looked around to see that he was inside a parking lot at a high-rise apartment building.

"You live here?"

"Yeah!" Erica answered as she climbed out of the car. "Come on!"

Gabe followed her from the rental and into the building. He rode with her on the elevator to the eleventh floor, and then followed her once the doors opened.

"This you, huh?" Gabe asked, looking around impressed.

"It's actually mine and a friend's," she admitted after unlocking the door and pushing it open.

Gabe turned around to see who was talking, only to pause and stare. He was caught up staring into the light, golden brown eyes of a woman whom he didn't even hear Erica introduce. He snapped out of his daze when she grabbed his arm.

"Yeah!" he answered, snapping out of his stare and looking at Erica.

"I said this is my sister, Brianna," Erica re-introduced her to Gabe.

"So, you the dude I hear was put in the hospital by my sister!" Brianna stated, while looking over Gabe, impressed by what she saw.

"You two sisters, huh?" Gabe asked, noticing that Erica had a mocha complexion while Brianna had golden honey skin.

Her honey blonde and brown hair reminded Gabe of the urban supermodel Jessica Rabbit.

"We're half-sisters," Brianna announced. "Same mom, different dad."

"That explains the look!" he told her as they held each other's eyes.

"Umm, Brianna!" Erica spoke up, interrupting what she saw was going on between her sister and Gabe. "You said you had to talk to me about something."

"Yeah!" Brianna answered, tearing her eyes away from Gabe to focus on her sister. "Let's go back to your bedroom real quick"

"Gabe, I'll be right back," Erica told him.

"You mind if I use ya phone?" Gabe asked, seeing her point to the wall phone inside the kitchen.

* * *

Once they got into Erica's bedroom, Brianna shut the door and locked it. She then pulled out a black backpack from under Erica's bed and tossed it on top of it.

"I need you to hold on to this for me until I come back for it!" Brianna told her sister.

"Do I wanna know what's in there, Brianna?" Erica asked, eyeing the backpack.

"Relax!" Brianna told her sister with a smirk. "It's only pills!"

Erica shook her head as she grabbed the backpack from the bed. She then walked over to her closet, only to hear Brianna ask, "So, what's up with Gabe?"

"What do you mean?"

"I mean, he's sexy! Does he have a woman?"

"I don't know, Brianna!" Erica replied. "What happened to Anthony?"

"Who?"

Erica shook her head at her sister and then walked over to open the room door, looking back over her shoulder.

"Brianna, I don't know a lot about Gabe, but I really don't think he's your type."

Brianna watched her sister walk out of the bedroom and smiled to herself.

"Well, I think her ass is dead wrong!"

* * *

Erica walked into the den and found Gabe and the puppy on the couch together watching ESPN news.

"Did you make your phone call?" she interrupted.

"Yeah!" Gabe answered. "I couldn't get anybody. But do you think you can give me a ride home? I'll pay for gas."

"I'm actually leaving now," Brianna announced as she walked into the den. "If you want a ride, I got you."

"Where you headed?" Gabe asked.

"I live in Miami," Brianna told him.

"That's where I'm going," Gabe stated as he picked up the puppy and stood up from his spot on the couch.

"You gonna write down ya number so we can keep in touch?" Gabe asked Erica.

* * *

Brianna waited for Gabe in the parking lot in her 2015 Mercedes-Benz ML63. She picked up her phone once it began ringing and saw it was her supposed boyfriend who she was about to cut loose. She was just about to answer the call, when she looked up to see Gabe walking his sexy ass out of Erica's building. Brianna ignored Anthony's phone call, hit the window button, and called out to Gabe. She then unlocked her car door as he walked over and climbed into the truck.

"Good look, ma!" Gabe thanked her as he was shutting the passenger door.

"It's cool, handsome!" Brianna replied as she pulled off. "Where we going?"

Gabe gave Brianna the address to his father's house. He then looked down at the puppy, which was pulling his shirt out of her mouth after chewing on it. Brianna then asked Gabe the name of the dog, and he sat thinking a few moments.

"It's Duchess!"

"Duchess, huh?" Brianna repeated, causing the puppy to give a bark in reply to her. "I think she agrees to it."

Gabe rubbed Duchess's back, which caused her to lie down in his lap. He then looked over at Brianna.

"So, where you from?"

"Where you're taking me!"

"You may live there now, but you not from Miami. I hear an accent when you speak."

"You got one too. Where you from?"

"Is this how things gonna be between us?" she

97

asked, looking over at Gabe. "I ask a question and you answer with one of your own?"

Gabe lightly laughed and answered her question: "I'm from Chicago."

"You far away from home, sexy!"

"I know!"

"You living with family out here?"

"Pops and his family," Gabe told her. "How about you? What you mixed with?"

"Mom's Italian and my dad was Jamaican," she responded, before turning the conversation back to him. "How old are you, sexy?"

"I'll be eighteen in a few weeks."

"Eighteen, huh?" she repeated in surprise. "You act like someone older than seventeen turning eighteen! You got a woman, handsome?"

Gabe smirked as he looked back over at Brianna.

"Yeah! I just started seeing someone."

"Too bad!" Brianna said with a smile. "I actually was looking forward to having my way with your young fine ass!"

Gabe shook his head and chuckled. He decided right there and then that he liked Brianna in more ways than one.

* * *

Brianna arrived at Gabe's father's house and

98

dropped him off, and she gave.him her cell phone number to call her when he ended things with Shantae. She also refused his gas money. Gabe let himself inside the house and went straight up to his bedroom to strip out of the clothes he was wearing and jump in the shower.

He spent five minutes in the shower and then got out and dried off. He put on his boxers and wifebeater and then headed back to his bedroom with Duchess following behind. Once he was in his room standing at his closet, he pulled out a pair of metallic blue Polo jeans, picked up his all-white, low-top Air Force Ones, and headed back to the bed to see Duchess lying in the middle watching him.

"Comfortable?" Gabe playfully asked the puppy as he was getting dressed.

After getting dressed, Gabe headed back downstairs and grabbed the cordless from the wall inside the kitchen. He then called Duke's number.

"Who this?"

"What's up, playboy?"

"What the fuck! Where the fuck you at, nigga?"

"I'm at the house. You at school?"

"Naw! I'm on my way to ya crib now," Duke

told him. "You do,know that Shantae is ready to fuck you up though, right?"

"I'll deal with Shantae when I see her," Gabe stated as he thought back to the phone call he overheard before the accident with Erica.

* * *

Duke left school right after he received Gabe's phone call, and arrived at his father's house ten minutes later. Duke parked the Explorer and saw Gabe sitting on the porch drinking orange juice.

"What's up, my nigga?" Duke questioned.

As Duke walked up to the porch and Gabe stood up, Duke instantly saw his boy's lip and the stitches above his right eyebrow.

"What the fuck happened to you?"

"It's nothing!" Gabe said, waving his hand dismissively. "I got something I wanna holla at you about."

"What up?" Duke asked as he and Gabe sat down back onto the porch.

Gabe explained to Duke what was on his mind since before the accident. He told his boy about them stepping up their game from robbing dope boys and switching to hitting jewelry stores. Gabe then told Duke about already having a guy who was willing to buy whatever jewelry he got.

"Bruh, that shit sounds good, but what about security and cameras?" Duke asked once Gabe was finished.

"I already thought of that too!" Gabe informed with a smirk. "You know the white boy Simon, at school? Well, dude supposed to be some type of computer genius from what I'm hearing."

"So how you plan on getting him to help us?" Duke asked.

Gabe slowly smiled at Duke, just as the barking started up. Gabe then leaned back and opened the front door to allow Duchess outside.

He shut the door and then said, "I'll deal with Simon. You with me or not?"

"That's not even a question!" Duke answered, before he nodded to Duchess as she walked around in of the front yard. "Where'd you get the puppy?"

"She found me!" Gabe answered.

He whistled, which caused Duchess to take off running and head straight back to him.

G abe kept his word and got together the next day with Simon Parker at school. He walked up to the boy sitting by himself in the lunch room and offered him $1,000 to help him out with something. He explained to Simon that he would tell him more later. Gabe got a quick agreement to work together from Simon, and afterward he let Duke know about their new partner.

Gabe dealt with Shantae and her attitude toward him. He caught her home in her bedroom and forced her ass to chill. He then told her about his accident, which was why he was getting rides with Duke, and why he didn't call or talk with her at all the past few days. He also explained that he needed to get another phone since his other one was missing.

Gabe never mentioned to Shantae what he had heard on his phone between her and Silk, and she never brought it up either. So Gabe just left the whole thing alone and focused on his and Duke's next hit they would make as soon as he did some more research on the jewelry store in Aventura.

Gabe spent three days watching the store,

seeing how it was run and what time it closed. He sent Simon inside the store so he could see the security system, which gave him time to put his plan together to get into the store and pass the alarms and cameras.

Simon got back to Gabe two days later and let him know he was ready. Gabe then hit up Duke on his new Samsung Galaxy phone.

"Yo!"

"What up, playboy? You ready?"

Duke was quiet a moment and finally said, "Hell yeah! When we going on?"

"Tonight!" Gabe replied. "Meet me outside my pop's crib in two hours."

"I'm there!" Duke answered, before hanging up the phone.

* * *

Gabe stood outside at 1:00 a.m., approximately two hours from the time he last spoke with Duke. Gabe sat on the front porch smoking a Newport, when he noticed a black Porsche Boxster S pull up in front of his father's house. He saw Duke behind the wheel once the window went down.

Gabe grabbed his dark blue backpack, walked over to the passenger side, and climbed into the car.

"What's up, my nigga?" Duke said, dapping up with Gabe.

"What up?" Gabe replied as he looked around the porch. "I'm feeling the Porsche!"

"Me too!" Duke said, smiling as he pulled off from in front of the house. "So what's up with Simon? We picking him up or what?"

"Naw!" Gabe answered as he dug out his cell phone and punched in Simon's number.

"Hello!" Simon answered after two rings.

"It's me!" Gabe said. "We headed to the spot now. You ready?"

"I'm already set up and just waiting on you and Duke."

"A'ight! I'ma hit you back once we get there!" Gabe informed him, before hanging up the phone. He then looked over at Duke. "Everything's ready. Simon is set up and is waiting for us."

"Where the fuck is he at?"

"At his house!"

"What?"

"He hacked into the security system and the jewelry store's computer from the safety of his own bedroom. That's part of the deal I made with him. He doesn't want to be on the scene when we're working!" Gabe said with a chuckle.

Duke shook his head and smiled. He hit the gas harder, which caused the Porsche to kick up speed.

* * *

Duke pulled down the street on which the jewelry store was located. He intentionally passed it to get a look around and to make sure it was closed and empty. Duke then turned the Porsche around and drove back up the street, but parked across the street from the store.

When Duke heard Gabe talking, he looked over and saw him on the phone with whom he guessed was Simon.

"Let's go!" Gabe told Duke, speaking over the phone's mouthpiece.

Duke and Gabe climbed from the Porsche and jogged across the street with their masks in place. Duke was shocked as hell when Gabe pulled the door straight open with no problem at all.

"What the fuck!" Duke exclaimed as he followed Gabe into the dark store.

He heard Gabe say something about display lights and froze in place when every light on the glass display case lit up, showing the jewelry and whatever else was inside the cases.

"Get to work!" Duke heard Gabe call out, catching the backpack he tossed to him before jogging off.

Gabe left Duke up front and ran to the back of the store where the safe was. He spotted it instantly since it took up half the wall.

"Simon, what's up?"

"Gimme a second!" Simon replied. "I'm almost done with the combination code. There! It's open, Gabe!"

Gabe looked back at the safe just as the door popped open a crack. Gabe smiled as he walked over and pulled open the door and stepped inside. The safe lit up, and he found himself looking at gold and diamonds the size of this thumb.

"Hell fucking yeah!"

* * *

Duke and Gabe rushed out of the store ten minutes later with two bags filled with everything they had laid eyes on. Duke hopped back in the driver's seat and had the engine started by the time Gabe was back in the passenger seat with both bags in his lap. Duke flew away from in front of the jewelry store. He smiled as he looked over at Gabe, who was on the phone with Simon.

"Where we going?" Duke asked as soon as Gabe hung up the phone.

Gabe remained quiet for a moment and then looked at his watch. It was almost three o'clock in the morning.

"Let's put this shit at your spot until later, and then we'll hook up with my nigga, Paul."

G abe woke up early that Friday morning since it was his birthday. He got in his normal workout and jogged a few miles before he had to get ready for school. He made it back to his father's house to find Nicole already up and cooking breakfast.

"Hey, sweetheart!" Nicole said, smiling as he kissed her cheek.

"You're up early!" Gabe stated as he got a glass of water and then leaned back against the counter beside Nicole.

"Today's your birthday, so I thought I'd get up and fix you breakfast," Nicole admitted with a smile.

She looked over as David walked into the kitchen and slowed when he saw Gabe. Gabe paused when he saw the look on his father's face, so he set down his glass and kissed Nicole on the cheek.

"I'ma take a shower," Gabe said.

"Okay, sweetie," Nicole said, smiling as she stood watching Gabe leave the kitchen while ignoring the way her husband was staring at her.

Gabe heard his father crank up as soon as he

left the kitchen. He shook his head as he left to go upstairs to his bedroom, only to run into his brother Aaron. He could see his brother tilt his body to lean into him, but Gabe shifted his body left and swung and smashed a left hook to Aaron's side, knocking the breath out of him.

Gabe watched Aaron fall to his knees holding his side and trying to catch his breath. Gabe then saw tears fall down his step-brother's face. He shook his head as he turned and walked off and headed toward his bedroom.

Gabe walked into his bedroom a few moments later and was greeted by Duchess, who sat up in his bed when she saw him.

"Hey, baby girl!" Gabe said, smiling as he walked over to the bed and picked up the dog.

He kissed her on the nose and received a lick in return.

Gabe heard his cell phone ring from inside his sweatpants pocket. He used his right hand and dug out the phone, to see that Brianna was calling.

"What's good, Brianna?" Gabe answered as he put down Duchess and walked over to his closet.

"What's up, birthday boy? How's your birthday going so far?"

"It's good so far. What's up with you though?

Why am I just now hearing from you when I called you weeks ago?"

"Damn! I ain't know you was my man already. But if you must know, I've been handling business, Gabriel, and I've see you a few times around the city with the cute boy driving the Explorer."

"Cute, huh?"

"You jealous?"

"Do I have a reason to be?"

"Yeah! So says your lips."

"If I say something, then that's the only truth to it."

"But anyway, I called to tell you I bought you a gift. What school you say you go to again?"

"Miami Norland Senior High. Why?"

"Just be where I can see you by lunchtime, handsome."

Gabe shook his head after Brianna hung up the phone on him, after she said what she had to say. He then tossed his phone onto the dresser and got ready for school.

* * *

Gabe was dressed in a Gucci suit and peanut butter brown Timberlands. He was standing on the sidewalk in front of the house after finishing the breakfast Nicole had prepared, when Duke called and said he was on his way. He was surprised when Shantae pulled up instead in her Mustang.

"Surprised to see me?" she asked, smiling from the driver's window. "Come on! Let's go so I can show you something!"

Gabe walked out to her Mustang and hopped in the passenger seat. He received a kiss from Shantae before she pulled off smiling the whole time.

"So, where we headed?" Gabe asked, a few minutes after they left his father's house.

"You'll see!" Shantae told him with a smile as she picked up an already rolled blunt and handed it to Gabe.

Gabe accepted it and smoked the blunt while relaxing back in his seat until Shantae turned toward the Miami Gardens area. She then swung the Mustang down a neighborhood street with a tall black steel security gate. Gabe watched as Shantae punched in a gate code to open it.

"Who lives here?" Gabe asked, looking around at the gated community he first thought was apartments, but were houses and townhomes.

Shantae refused to answer Gabe's questions even after parking in the driveway of a cream-and-brown-colored, two-story townhome. She shut off the car and then got out. She then called to Gabe to also get out of the car.

"So you're just refusing to answer me now, right?" Gabe asked, after getting out of the Mustang and following Shantae to the front door of the townhome.

"Just wait!" she told him, using the key on her ring to unlock the front door.

She pushed open the door and grabbed Gabe's hand, dragging him inside behind her.

Shantae showed Gabe through the fully furnished two-story, two-bedroom, one-and-a-half bath home. She finished the tour after leading Gabe from the sizeable kitchen out onto the back patio with a nine-foot pool.

"What do you think?"

"Whose spot is this, Shan?" he asked again.

"It's ours, nigga! Damn!" she said, sucking her teeth.

"Ours!"

"That's what I said!"

"I'ma need a little more than that, Shan!"

She sucked her teeth again and explained to him how Kiki and her baby daddy got a place there, and she told Shantae how affordable it was, so she got a place for the both of them.

"Now, do you like it or not, boy?" she asked,

folding her arms across her chest and staring hard at him.

Gabe laughed at how Shantae was looking at him. He leaned over and kissed her on the lips and said, "Yeah, ma! I like it!"

Shantae smiled upon hearing Gabe's approval, and she threw her arms around his neck and kissed him directly on his lips. She felt his arms slide around her waist until his hands gently gripped her ass. She then stepped closer into him until their bodies pressed together.

* * *

Gabe and Shantae made it to school just before the school bell rang. They went their own ways after Shantae took another kiss and then jogged off, with Gabe simply shaking his head and smiling. He then headed off to his own class, stepping inside the room just as his cell phone began vibrating from inside his pocket.

He found a seat and pulled out his phone, seeing that he had a text message from Brianna, along with an attachment. Gabe opened the picture first and almost dropped his phone.

"Damn!" Gabe whispered to himself.

He then stared at the butt-ass naked picture of Brianna wearing a "Happy Birthday, Bitch!" hat on her head. She was blowing a kiss at the camera. He couldn't help thinking how sexy she looked, and his dick immediately got hard as steel. He thought good-looking Brianna looked even better naked.

Gabe saved the picture and then opened the text message, which was a happy birthday message letting him know that whenever he was ready, what he saw was all his. He sent back a quick text letting her know he would keep the offer in mind.

* * *

Gabe made it through the first half of the school day. He also ran into Boo Man and a few of the other new friends who had he made at school. Gabe left his fourth-period class once the bell rang, and he started for his lunch break. He headed outside to the back of the student parking lot and heard his name called. He turned around and saw Lisa and Kiki running to catch up with him.

"Hey, birthday boy!" Kiki cried as she and Lisa hugged him together.

He received a kiss from both girls, and was then escorted to the parking lot where Duke and Boo Man were standing with Melody.

"Hey, birthday boy!" Melody said with a smile as she walked up to Gabe and hugged him and then gave him a kiss on the cheek.

After receiving hugs and embraces from the rest of the crew, he noticed that Shantae was missing. He asked where she was as he turned around and looked in every direction.

"We thought she was with you!" Duke told him, looking around now and mentioning that Silk was also missing.

Gabe saw both Shantae's and Silk's rides still parked in the lot, so he pulled out his cell phone to call her. But his phone rang in his hand that instant as he saw that Brianna was calling.

"What's up, Brianna?"

"Where you at, handsome?"

"School!"

"Where at exactly, Gabriel?"

"Back end! Student parking lot."

"Walk out to the street."

After hearing Brianna hang up on him again, Gabe shook his head and told his friends that he was going to be right back. He walked off and headed to the exit, when he noticed the distant sound of music and heavy bass.

"What the fuck!" Gabe said in disbelief as he saw Brianna's Benz truck turning down the street, followed by the 2008 Escalade EXT that was blaring Rick Ross's "Pushing It" from its system.

Both the Benz and Escalade stopped in front of him and the music was turned down, but Gabe could still feel the bass. He stood watching as a red-bone female with a body that should be on the cover of *Straight Stuntin Magazine* climbed from the Escalade's driver's seat. She walked over to Gabe and gave him a kiss on his cheek and wished him a happy birthday, before she walked around to the passenger side of the Benz truck.

Gabe then shifted his eyes to the driver's window to see the window drop down and Brianna smile at him. He then started to walk over to the car.

"What's up, ma?"

"You tell me, daddy!" Brianna replied flirtatiously. "You like your gifts?"

"You mean the picture and a visit from you, right?" Gabe asked, flirting right back.

He gently ran the back of his hand down the side of Brianna's face, which caused her body to give a quick but very noticeable shiver. She closed her eyes for a moment, and then a smile appeared on her lips.

"Oh, so you wanna tease a bitch now, huh?" Brianna said, still smiling. "Just wait till I get my hands on your ass!"

"You may not be ready for—!"

"What the hell!" Brianna said, cutting off Gabe and looking past him at a fight about to pop off.

Gabe heard a scream and his name being called. He spun around to see Melody, Duke, and the others take off running across the parking lot. He heard more yelling, and then saw Silk and Shantae going to blows fighting at the back entrance of the school.

"Gabriel!" Brianna yelled as he dropped his backpack and took off running back into the parking lot.

* * *

People saw another side of Gabe as he pushed through the crowd of students and even knocked down a few of them until he broke through the crowd. He rushed straight over to the guy fighting the female, who was putting up quite a fight herself. Brianna was shocked as hell at how hard Gabe hit the guy. In fact, she could see the blood fly from his face from her car, and what looked like meat hanging from his right cheek. Gabe hit him again until he dropped on the steps.

"Shit!" Brianna yelled, seeing Gabe begin stomping the guy.

She jumped out of the car along with her friend, Sherry, and the both of them rushed into the parking lot.

By the time the two of them reached Gabe and the guy he was stomping in the face with his Tims, Brianna grabbed Gabe to stop him from really messing the guy up.

"Gabriel! Baby, it's me, Brianna!"

Once Gabe heard Brianna's name and saw her face, he broke the zone he was in and looked at Silk, who was fucked up badly and lying motionless on the ground. He spun around to see Duke and Melody with Shantae, and he couldn't help notice the way she looked.

"Duke, get Shantae to the house. I'ma catch y'all later!"

"Gabe, where are you going?" Shantae yelled as he ran off with the two women who stopped the fight.

All Shantae could do was watch him as he jumped into a root-beer-colored Escalade pulling off behind a pear metallic Mercedes-Benz truck.

13

Shantae was worried beyond explaining the longer she sat waiting for Gabe to call or come home like he had promised. She tried ignoring the fact that her man was out with some woman she heard call him baby, so she tried to focus on what Duke and Boo Man were talking about after Melody called with information on Silk after he was taken to the hospital.

Shantae then got up from the couch to go into the kitchen for something to drink. She heard the sound of a big engine pulling up and took off to the front door. She snatched open the handle and saw the truck in which Gabe had driven off. She walked out to the Escalade just as he was getting out.

"Gabe, where have you been? Are you alright?"

"I'm good!" Gabe answered as he walked right past Shantae and headed for the front door of the townhome, only for her to stop him.

"That's it, nigga?" she asked as she got in his face. "I been here waiting for hours for your ass thinking the police picked you up or something bad happened, and all you gotta say when you get here is that you're good?"

"Pretty much!" Gabe replied, before he walked around her and entered the home.

"What's up, my nigga?" Duke said as soon as Gabe walked inside. "You good?"

"Shit! I think I broke my fucking hand on that nigga's jaw!" Gabe told his boys as he dropped onto the couch and accepted a blunt from Boo Man. "What you niggas heard about that bitch-ass nigga?"

"Truthfully, my nigga," Duke started, looking at Boo Man and then back at Gabe, "bruh, you fucked that dude up bad. His jaw is broke and the corner of his right eye socket is broke or chipped, or whatever Melody said the doctor told her. And the nigga's got a concussion. We not gonna talk about his cheek and his nose!"

"I should have broken the bitch nigga's neck!" Gabe stated, before he looked over at Shantae.

"Broke his neck for what, Gabe? You beat the boy up, that was enough. You didn't have to stomp the boy's face in, in front of the whole school!"

Gabe stared at Shantae a few moments before he began to chuckle and shake his head.

"I guess it's clear who the fuck your loyalty is to now, huh?"

"What the fuck is that supposed to mean?" Shantae yelled. "Nigga, your ass is my fucking man, so why would my loyalty be elsewhere?"

"So when was you planning on telling me about that little confession from that clown-ass nigga Silk?" Gabe asked, seeing Shantae's facial expression instantly change. "Yeah! You didn't think I knew about that argument you and that nigga had, huh? I just never said anything because I wanted to see if you would tell me; but I guess we know the answer to that, don't we?"

"Whoa!" Duke spoke up. "What are you talking about, my nigga?"

"Ask ya sister!" Gabe told him as he stood up from his seat. "Maybe she'll keep it gangsta with you, since she can't with me!"

"Gabe, wait!" Shantae yelled as she grabbed his arm, only for him to snatch it away when he walked out the front door.

Shantae stood staring at the front door after he walked out. She then heard the truck start up a few minutes later and drive away.

* * *

Gabe drove around after leaving Shantae,

Duke, and Boo Man at the townhome. He thought about the decision he made, letting her worry about his feelings. He didn't know if he could trust her after she couldn't tell him about something as simple as another guy wanting to take his place. Gabe then wondered, if things were more serious, who would Shantae really be down for? He pulled out his cell phone as he drove the Escalade, and hit speed dial for Brianna's number.

"Where you at, Gabriel?" Brianna asked, answering the phone at the start of the second ring.

"Where you at?" Gabe asked. "I'm trying to see you."

"Come to my place," Brianna told him, giving Gabe her address. "How long you gonna take to get here?"

"Not long!" he replied, hanging up the phone afterward.

* * *

Brianna was a little surprised to receive Gabe's call. She was suddenly nervous now that he was on his way over to her penthouse, because she remembered the sound of his voice when he told her he wanted to see her. She rushed to take a quick shower before he arrived, and was just drying off when the doorman downstairs called up to announce his arrival. She then told the doorman to let him up as she rushed to get herself together.

She put on a matching pink-and-white boy short and bra set, a pair of cotton short shorts that she knew hugged her ass, and a wifebeater. She then heard the doorbell ring and Eddie, her live-in servant, answer the door.

Brianna took a deep breath to calm her nerves. It surprised her at how the boy made her so nervous. She left her bedroom and started for the stairs, just as Eddie was coming up.

"Ms. Scott!"

"I know, Eddie!" she told him, not allowing the servant to finish. "Thank you, and you can have the rest of the night off."

"Thank you, ma'am," Eddie replied, smiling as he turned and walked away.

Brianna continued down the stairs and saw Gabe standing at the door looking at a picture of her next to it. He must have heard her, because he turned those green eyes on her and a small smile appeared on her lips.

"Hey, handsome! What's in the bag?"

"Food for us!" Gabe answered, holding up the two dinners he had picked up from Granny B's.

"We can eat in the den," she told Gabe, motioning for him to follow her.

Gabe sat down on the fur-like sofa in front of the floor-to-ceiling wide-screen TV and looked around at how put together the penthouse was. He then handed Brianna the white plastic bag with the two dinners.

"You got a nice place!" he added.

"Thank you!" Brianna replied as she set down a plate of food in front of Gabe.

She gave him the fried chicken wings and rib tips meal, while she took the fried fish and shrimp for herself.

Gabe looked around the room after Brianna had left the den and returned with four bottles of Heineken, two for him and two for her. He started in on his food, but mentioned something about a homeboy he saw in the picture with Brianna on the glass stand.

"He's nobody!" Brianna said, glancing over at the photo Gabe was talking about.

"If he's nobody, why is his picture up there?" Gabe asked back.

"His name is Anthony," she told him, staring

at Gabe. "We were together until recently."

"Recently, huh?"

"Yeah, recently!" Brianna repeated. "I can't trust him or shit he says, which means I can't be with his ass either. Period!"

Gabe nodded his head in understanding and went back to eating.

"So, what happened with you and the young girl you fought for? She alright?" Brianna asked.

"She good!"

"That's it? She good, Gabriel?"

"That's what I said, isn't it?" he asked, shooting her a look.

Brianna threw up her hands and said, "I take it you two must have got into a fight, right?"

"I broke off with her, Brianna!" he told her, tossing his fork onto his plate as he looked back at her. "I can't trust her. It's crazy, because I'm feeling shorty, but I really feel like her loyalty isn't with me; and if I keep fucking with her, I'ma end up getting fucked up in the end, and I can't have that."

"So, what now, Gabriel?" Brianna asked. "What are your plans?"

"What you mean?"

"Why are you here, Gabriel?" she asked as

she turned to face him. "You know already I want your young ass, but I'm not about to be your fallback girl. If you're here for pity or to use me to fill in for that girl or even for sex, then you know where the door is, boo! I don't do sidekicks or fuck buddies."

Gabe laughed lightly as he shook his head. He then turned back to his food and picked up his fork.

Brianna watched Gabe a few moments while he said nothing. He simply sat and ate his food. She hated being ignored, only to see him just sitting beside her saying nothing and stuffing his face.

"You know what, Gabriel! It's time for you to go!" she stood up and announced.

"Sit down, Brianna," he told her as he continued eating his food.

"Nigga, you think I'm playing?" Brianna asked, raising her voice. "Nigga, pack that shit up and get the fuck—!"

"Shut the fuck up with that shit!" Gabe barked at Brianna, catching her off guard as he shot to his feet. "I heard what the fuck you said, but the first thing that needs to be understood is that if I'ma be fucking with you, I ain't gonna be with all that kicking a nigga out and catching an attitude. The first time I catch you lying to me, we got a problem. Now sit down and eat before this food gets cold!"

Brianna was smiling by the time Gabe sat back down and continued eating. She did as her man had told her to and sat down back on the sofa. She looked back over at him, though, before starting to eat herself.

"Umm, there's one more thing you should know, Mr. Rule Layer!"

"What's that?" Gabe asked, cutting his eyes back over to Brianna.

"I expect my man to be in the same house as I'm in!" Brianna told him in all seriousness. "I wanna wake up next to my man in the morning and lay down beside him at night. Each night! Do you have a problem with that?"

Gabe chuckled as he shook his head. He then turned back to his food.

"You may wanna get something on before we leave to get my shit from pop's house," he said, right before he began eating again.

Brianna smiled after hearing her man's words. She then turned her attention to her food, trying to control her nervous excitement.

14

Brianna helped Gabe move out of his father's house and got to meet Nicole Green, his step-mother; and his protective puppy, Duchess. But she noticed that besides not saying anything about his father, he had nothing to say about his step-brothers as well. Brianna called a few friends who she trusted and had them over to her place to help get Gabe settled in, since she was planning to take her man out shopping for a few things that she felt he needed or even really wanted.

She introduced Gabe to Lorenzo, Tamara, and a smiling Sherry, who he had already met on his birthday and from whom he had received a hug and kiss on the cheek. Brianna took the time to sit Gabe down and explain a few things to him concerning exactly what she was into.

"Babe, look! I need you to understand what's going on with me!" Brianna began, getting his full attention as she, Gabe, Lorenzo, Sherry, and Tamara sat down in the den in her penthouse.

She broke down to Gabe her business with selling pills, and she even had a few different businesses that were selling molly pills for her. Brianna then explained the importance of them both being careful about letting too many people know where they lived. She explained a few more things about her business, and ended with offering Gabe a position with her in her business.

"I'm good, ma!" Gabe told her as he dug out a fresh pack of Newports from his pocket. "I already got a little something going on!"

"You gonna tell me what?" Brianna asked him as she took the cigarette Gabe offered to her.

Gabe took a pull from the Newport and blew the smoke toward the ceiling as Duchess hopped into his lap.

He shifted his eyes to Brianna and said, "Let's just say that I get my cash from muscle."

"You rob?" Lorenzo asked him.

When Brianna saw the smirk return to Gabe's face, she grabbed his hand and pulled him up. She then started leading him out of the den to the outside terrace. She shut the sliding glass door behind her and then turned to face Gabe.

"Gabe, listen, babe! I can't tell you what to do, because you're a grown-ass man; but as a favor to me, I'm asking you to leave that robbing stuff alone. Please!"

"Leave it alone!" Gabe repeated, but then asked, "Leave it alone and do what, Brianna?

Find a job, ma?"

"I'll give you a position, Gabriel!"

"I don't need you to give me anything! You've already bought that truck downstairs, and the only reason I accepted that was because it's a gift for my birthday!"

"Hold up!" Brianna said with an attitude as she stared at Gabe with her hands on her hips. "You telling me that if I want to buy my man something, I can't?"

"What I'm saying is that I don't need handouts, ma!" Gabe explained. "I ain't never needed nobody to give me nothing, and I ain't gonna allow the shit now. If you wanna do something for me, then do it because you just wanna gift ya man with something. Don't do it because it's on some pity shit!"

"Wait a fucking second, nigga!" Brianna said, jabbing Gabe in his chest with her finger. "Muthafucker, I don't run no charity up in here, and if I felt like you wasn't on nothing, you wouldn't be up in this shit. Yeah, you young, but I see something in your young ass that I want in my life. So if you got a problem with accepting gifts from me, then get over it, because if I see something I want you to have, then you're getting it. And as a matter of fact, we're about to go to the mall because I'ma take you out for your birthday. Do you have a problem with that, Gabriel Green?"

Gabe stared directly into Brianna's cat-brown eyes and couldn't help but smile as he reached out and grabbed her by her forty-five-inch phat ass. He pulled her up against him and leaned in to kiss her on the lips, and he could feel her instantly respond to the kiss.

* * *

Shantae lay across the bed inside her new townhome that was supposed to be for her and Gabe. But now she was all alone because her man didn't think he could trust her. She gripped her cell phone in her hand and stared at the TV, even though she wasn't watching it. She thought about Silk and the condition he was now in, all because of the fight she and he were in, only to have Gabe interrupt and really hurt her best friend.

Shantae made the decision and called Silk's sister to check and see how he was doing. She sat listening to the line ring two and then three times, when it was finally picked up on the fourth ring.

"Hello!"

"Brenda, it's Shantae!"

"Hey, Shantae. Why aren't you at the hospital with Kevin? He's been asking about you."

"Is he up now?"

"Me and my momma just left the hospital, but Boo Man, Melody, and Gina are still there with him."

"Was my brother there?"

"Girl, neither you nor Duke showed up! Are you going to see him?"

"Yes!" Shantae answered, before she thought about it and as she climbed off her bed. "I'ma get out there now. What room and floor is he on?"

Once Shantae found out the hospital and room number, she hung up and got dressed to go see her friend. She rushed out the front door a few minutes after she was done. Once she got in her Mustang, she thought about calling Gabe, but she decided against it. Instead, she thought she'd call him after she first went to visit Silk.

* * *

Gabe kicked it with Brianna and her crew, but he mostly hung back with Lorenzo while Brianna, Sherry, and Tamara took control of the shopping he was supposed to be doing. Gabe found himself giving his approval to a few outfits, and noticed that Brianna and Tamara had a thing for matching up his shoes and fitted hats with the clothes they were picking out for hm.

"I want to get your ears pierced!" Brianna told Gabe at one point while dragging him into a tattoo shop.

They went back and forth until she got what she wanted, which was getting Gabe to give in and agree to get his ears pierced. However, while there, Brianna was going to get his name tattooed on her lower back right above her ass.

After the tattoos and the ear piercing were finished, Gabe left with new white diamond studs, while Brianna left with a new tattoo of her man's name across her lower back.

"Gabriel, don't make me have to fuck you up about ever playing with me!" Brianna told him after they left the tattoo shop. "I got this tattoo, so you belong to me, just as I belong to you. So don't act crazy, boy!"

"You got me, ma!" Gabe told her with a smile as he dropped his arm around her shoulders. "I ain't going nowhere as long as you keep it a hundred with me!"

"Ummm, excuse me!" Sherry spoke up as she slowed up and fell back from Lorenzo and Tamara to walk with Brianna and Gabe. "It's almost 7:00 p.m., and we're hungry, girl! We trying to go to Aunt I's to get some seafood!"

"You hungry, baby?" Brianna asked as Gabe dug out his ringing phone.

"I can eat something," Gabe replied as he saw Duke's name appear on his phone.

"What's good, playboy?" Gabe said.

"What's up, my nigga? Where you at?"

"I'm at the mall right now. What's good though?"

"I wanna talk to you about some business," Duke told him. "Can you meet me at my mom's house real quick?"

Gabe told Duke to hold on as he looked back and interrupted Brianna, Sherry, and Tamara.

"Bri!"

"Yeah!" Brianna answered, turning back toward Gabe.

Gabe explained what was just said between him and Duke; however, he didn't want to get too deep into what his boy wanted to holla at him about. Gabe never got to finish, because Brianna turned to her friends and told them that they would meet them at Aunt I's Soul Food House after they handled something.

Gabe got back on the phone with Duke and let

his boy know he was on his way. He hung up the phone, and after saying goodbye to Lorenzo, Sherry, and Tamara, he and Brianna broke off from the others and headed toward the exit.

Once they were outside and walking toward the parking lot, Brianna gave Gabe the two bags she was carrying that went with the eight bags he was carrying. She got into the front passenger seat, on the custom Louis Vuitton upholstered seats, and waited until Gabe climbed behind the wheel and started up the truck.

"Gabriel, I'ma say something, but I don't want you to take this the wrong way!"

"I'm listening!"

"I really wish you would leave this robbing stuff alone! It really bothers me that you're out here doing this."

"Why's it bothering you?"

"Because!" Brianna stated with a sigh. "My father used to do the same thing you're out in the streets doing, and he ended up dead, Gabriel! I just found you, and I'm really not trying to lose you the same way!"

Gabe sighed softly but deeply as he glanced back over at Brianna and saw the pleading expression she had on her face.

"A'ight, Bri! I'ma do this shit for you. But you do know that I could easily get fucked up selling pills or whatever, just as I would doing what I'm already doing."

"Yeah, I understand that, but you have better chances my way than yours!"

"Yeah! Well, you gonna have to break down all this shit to me, you know!"

Brianna smiled as she leaned over toward Gabe and first kissed his neck and then his lips. She reached between his legs and gripped his manhood, smiling at the size and weight.

"I've got a lot I want to teach you, sexy! Trust me!" she said.

15

Duke was sitting out on the porch smoking a blunt, when he saw the Escalade EXT truck turn down his street and roll up the block to slow down in front of his mother's house. He looked over the truck and was staring at the thirty-inch chrome Forgiato rims and brushed wheels. He continued watching as the passenger window slid down and he saw Gabe and a bad-ass female in the passenger seat. Duke stood up from the porch rail on which he was sitting and headed out to the truck, walking up to the passenger window.

"What's up, playboy?" Gabe said as Duke leaned in to the passenger window.

"What's good, my nigga?"

"Bri, this my nigga Duke!" Gabe introduced, seeing the look Duke gave Brianna. "So what's up? You say you got a hit for us?"

"Yeah!" Duke answered, but cut his eyes over to Brianna and then looked back at Gabe.

"Relax, playboy!" Gabe told his boy, smiling after catching the way Duke looked at Brianna. "This my lady! She good, and I trust her, so talk!"

Duke was caught off guard to hear Gabe say the girl in front of him was his girlfriend. But considering what had happened between Shantae and Gabe, Duke left the issue alone.

"A'ight, fuck it! You remember that shit with Hernandez, right?"

"Hell yeah!" Gabe exclaimed as he leaned over toward Brianna and stared at Duke outside the truck.

"I found out what happened to the Donk that you wanted his ass to fix up but suddenly was stolen!" Duke began to explain to Gabe.

He was just about to continue his story, when Brianna spoke up directly to Gabe: "Babe, which Hernandez y'all talking about? Fat Hernandez that got the auto and paint shop cross town?"

"Yeah!" Gabe answered. "Why? You know fool or something?"

"Who you think I bought you this truck from?" Brianna admitted. "I know Hernandez's ass since he works for me too!"

"Works for you?" Duke asked.

"Never mind that, playboy!" Gabe told his boy.

"Ma, I know we just talked and agreed that I would leave this shit alone, but this fool rubbed me for a '74 model Chevy Caprice convertible. I've been waiting on this clown, shorty!"

Brianna shook her head but understood her man's need.

"Alright, Gabriel. But this is the last time; and you've got to be careful because Hernandez always keeps guns on him, even when it doesn't seem like it. Also, I seen the Caprice you're talking about!"

"Where it at?" both Duke and Gabe said at the same time.

* * *

Shantae left the hospital after seeing Silk and felt better about the issue between the two of them. She respected the fact that he was still in love with her since they were kids. However, she confessed to him that she felt differently for him, but that at one point she did have feelings for him. Shantae tried calling Duke and got his voice message, so she just told him to call her back when he could.

After hanging up and calling Gabe, just as she was turning down the street that her mother lived on, she caught sight of a familiar truck a little ways up the street that was turning the corner at the end of the block. She hung up the phone once Gabe's voice message switched on, and she pulled up in front of her mother's house, only to see her brother climbing into his Explorer.

"Duke!" Shantae yelled from the passenger window after letting it down. She then watched as her brother backed out of the driveway and quickly pulled up beside her. "Where you about to go?"

"I gotta handle something real quick. Why? You a'ight?"

"Yeah! I just left from seeing Silk! He asked about you, Duke."

Duke shook his head.

"Shantae, tell me something. This the same muthafucker that was beating the fuck outta you before that nigga Gabe got in the middle of the shit? How you go to chill with that nigga but let that nigga Gabe go like that?"

"Duke, I ain't trying to get into it right now," Shantae stated, waving her hand dismissively. "You talked to Gabe? I been trying to call his ass, and he ain't answering the phone!"

"You not listening, is you?" Duke asked her. "I just told you a second ago the boy is gone, Shantae!"

"What are you talking about, Duke?" Shantae asked, truly confused.

Duke shook his head again.

"Shantae, when you let Gabe walk out of that townhouse earlier, you let that man leave! Period! He just left here a few minutes ago with his new girlfriend!"

Shantae stared at her brother in disbelief. In fact, she never really paid much attention to the fact that Duke had already driven off and left her sitting right where she was.

* * *

Gabe and Brianna hooked back up with Lorenzo, Sherry, and Tamara at the soul food seafood restaurant. But while the two of them ate dinner, their minds were both on something else. After they all had finished dinner and the five were ready to leave, Brianna pulled Lorenzo aside and talked with him for a few minutes, and then the two then rejoined the others.

"Bri!" Gabe called out, just as he hung up the phone.

"Baby, go handle your business. I'll ride with Sherry and Tamara, and I'll see you back at home," she spoke up before he could even say another word.

Brianna accepted the kiss Gabe gave her, and then she watched her man jog off toward his truck. She sighed deeply and loudly as the

Escalade drove off from the restaurant followed by Lorenzo's Aston Martin DB9.

* * *

Gabe met up with Duke right on the corner of Country Line Road at a Quicky Mart store as planned. Gabe parked the Escalade and then walked over to the Jeep Grand Cherokee SRT and climbed in the passenger seat.

"Here!" Duke said as he tossed a gray backpack over into Gabe's lap before cranking up the Jeep and pulling off.

Gabe unzipped the backpack and looked inside. He slowly smiled as he dug out the MAC-11 and the TEC-9. He checked the magazine on the MAC-11 and saw that it was fully loaded. He slid the magazine back in and sent a round into the chamber.

"Where's his ass at now?" Gabe finally asked, speaking softly but loud enough to be heard.

"I left his ass at this warehouse out in Fort Lauderdale!" Duke told Gabe. "He got like seven dudes with him. But, bruh, wait 'til you see what the fuck's inside this warehouse! It's crazy for real!"

Gabe remembered what Brianna had told him about Hernandez and the money he was making selling cars and other types of rides as well as entering car shows. Gabe wasn't surprised at what Duke was telling him, and was actually looking forward to what he was about to find once they reached this warehouse.

* * *

Shantae pulled up in front of Gabe's father's house and saw the four cars she remembered from the last time she visited to pick up Gabe. But she didn't see the truck Gabe was now driving. She made a decision and parked her Mustang, entered the front gate, and rang the front doorbell.

Shantae waited a few moments, when she finally heard the front door being unlocked and saw it swing wide open.

"Hi, I'm Shantae. Is Gabriel here?" Shantae asked with a big smile.

"I'm sorry, sweetheart," Nicole told the young lady. "My step-son no longer lives here."

"Do you know where he lives now, ma'am?"

"No, sweetheart. But I can call his girlfriend if you would like, and talk to her about Gabriel. He's not answering his phone right now."

"Please!"

"Hold on a second!"

Shantae waited out on the front porch as

Gabe's mother disappeared inside the house. Shantae stood there and played Gabe's mother's words over again inside her head: "His girlfriend!"

Once Mrs. Green reappeared with her cell phone in her hand, Shantae stood and listened as Gabe's mother stood talking to some woman named Brianna who was supposed to be Gabe's girlfriend. She continued to listen as Mrs. Green spoke both friendlily and freely with the other woman.

"Well, from what Brianna says, Shantae," Nicole started after hanging up the phone, "Gabriel is out in the streets with friends, but she said she will contact him and have him call me. If you want, I'll have Gabriel call you."

"Thank you!" Shantae stated, smiling as she said goodbye.

She started back out to her car, quickly losing her smile at the thought of Gabe and this Brianna bitch he was supposedly now seeing.

Once she got into her Mustang and sat behind the wheel, Shantae slammed her fist down against the steering wheel.

"This muthafucker!" she yelled out in anger and disbelief. "I'ma show this muthafucker about playing with me! I told his ass already before!"

* * *

Gabe and Duke didn't bother with creeping around the back once they reached the warehouse. They didn't care about all the noise the Jeep made as Duke pulled up in front. They both jogged straight up to the two sliding front doors to the warehouse just as they were being opened. Gabe let the MAC-11 speak out.

Brrrrrr!

Gabe cut down the dude's leg at the warehouse entrance as he led the way into the warehouse catching six other men frozen in place. They tried to break out in a run once they realized what was happening.

Tat, tat, tat, tat, tat, tat, tat!

Gabe watched all six of the remaining men drop to the ground after Duke let his TEC-9 blast off into the air. Gabe then shook his head as he looked around the warehouse and saw the different rides that were hooked up and sitting on everything from twenty-fives on up to thirty-twos. He then shifted his eyes over to fat-ass Hernandez as his punk ass laid facedown with both hands covering his head.

As Gabe walked over and stood in front of

Hernandez, he kicked him in the head.

"Get yo' punk ass up!"

"Gabe, just let me—!" Hernandez started.

"Get the fuck up!" Gabe barked, kicking Hernandez straight in the face. "I ain't trying to hear shit yo' ass gotta say. Get yo' bitch ass up!"

Gabe watched as Hernandez slowly got to his knees and slowly stood to his feet, when he heard Duke let off a blast of bullets from the TEC-9. Gabe spun around just in time to see one of the six guys running and taking off out of the warehouse with Duke right behind his ass.

When Gabe turned back to Hernandez and forced him back on his knees, he suddenly heard what sounded like a cannon going off two times and then once more outside the warehouse. Gabe glanced back toward the entrance and then back to Hernandez. He then looked around again when he heard Duke call out his name and saw him leading another guy into the warehouse.

"What the fuck!" Gabe said in surprise, after recognizing who Duke had at gunpoint. "Playboy, relax! That's family!"

"So this what you out here for, huh?" Lorenzo asked Gabe, once his homeboy lowered the TEC-9.

"What the fuck is you doing here, Zo?" Gabe asked him, watching as Lorenzo walked over to a '72 Chevy Impala.

"Ya wife sent me out here to watch ya back!" Lorenzo explained as he turned to the box Chevy Caprice '84 model that was sitting on twenty-eight-inch DUB skirts.

Gabe shook his head after hearing what Lorenzo told him about Brianna. But he then turned his focus back to Hernandez.

"Here's how this is gonna go! I'ma shut this shit down. But you, homeboy. You fucked with the wrong dude!"

As Gabe watched Hernandez open his mouth to explain, he swung up the MAC-11 and let the thing sing.

Brrrrrr! Brrrrrrr! Brrrrrr!

* * *

Brianna was waiting in the den for either Lorenzo's phone call or Gabe to walk through the door. She was really beginning to worry about her man, but she was trying not to overreact and start blowing up his phone like some controlling girlfriend.

Brianna heard the doorbell sound off, which caused Duchess to start barking and jump off the sofa beside her. Brianna followed the dog to the front door.

"Duchess, please!" Brianna scolded, trying to quiet the dog as she looked out the peephole to see her sister standing there.

She unlocked and opened the door.

"Hey, girl!" Erica said, walking past her sister, carrying a plastic bag and a drink.

She looked down and noticed a familiar dog.

"Brianna, whose dog is that?"

"Who you think?" Brianna asked, smirking as she closed and relocked the front door.

Brianna started toward the den calling Duchess behind her. She then sat down on the sofa with Duchess beside her as Erica sat down to her left. Brianna then picked up the TV remote just as Erica started with her questions.

"Brianna, what's going on? Why is Gabe's dog over here, and where is he?"

"You came over here to question me about Gabriel or to see me?"

"Actually, I came over because momma asked me to tell you that there's a family reunion tomorrow. She wants us to drive out to the house early to help with getting everything set up, and Darrell also said he needs to talk to you."

"About what?"

"Girl, I don't even—!"

Brianna heard the sound of the front door open, which interrupted Erica. Brianna controlled herself even though she wanted to leap from the sofa and rush to the front door. Instead, she stayed right where she was and waited until her man appeared in the doorway with Duchess under his left arm and a duffel bag in his right hand.

"What's up, Erica?" Gabe said, nodding to her as he tossed the duffel bag on the floor at Brianna's feet.

He then bent down and kissed her lips before sitting down beside her. He then lay outstretched across the sofa with his head in Brianna's lap.

"How'd everything go?" she asked as she rubbed her fingers through his curly hair that needed cutting.

"Everything went straight, and I even got a few apology gifts!" Gabe replied as he dug out two keys and handed them back over his head to Brianna and then tapped the duffel bag on the floor.

"What are the keys for?" Brianna asked, looking at them and seeing that one was to a Buick and the other for a Chevy.

"I'll show you in the morning!" he told her as he rolled onto his side and turned to face Brianna's stomach.

Gabe then wrapped his arm around her middle. Brianna smiled at the touch of Gabe's lips against her stomach as he kissed her. She rubbed the back of her man's head as she looked across the room at Erica, only to see her sister staring open-mouthed at her with a shocked look on her face.

16

G abe was up early as usual and down in the building's garage with Duke and Lorenzo. They were looking at the two new rides they took from Hernandez's warehouse the night before. Gabe was looking under the hood of the oriental-blue-painted 1975 Buick LeSabre with the blue ragtop Asanti grille, suicide doors, and halo headlights. He looked up after hearing Lorenzo call out his name from over near the 1974 Chevy Caprice convertible that was supposedly stolen, but was now in perfect condition.

Gabe saw Lorenzo nod in the direction of the elevator and saw Brianna walking in their direction dressed in pink and white cotton sweatpants that hugged her lower body perfectly. She also had on a matching pink and white Nike top. He couldn't help smiling at just the simple sight of his lady.

"Hey, sexy!" Brianna said as she walked up on Gabe and kissed him on the lips. "Why didn't you wake me up when you got up?"

"You looked tired!" Gabe told her as Lorenzo and Duke walked up.

"What's up, Brianna?" Duke spoke up in

greeting.

"Hey, Duke!" Brianna said with a little wave before she looked back over at Gabe. "Babe, what you gonna do? My mom is having a family reunion, and I was already supposed to have left for it. You coming with me, right?"

"Momma cooking her honey ham?" Lorenzo asked, smiling over at Brianna.

"Boy, I don't know!" she answered, shaking her head at him before looking over at Duke. "You can come too, if you want."

"What time you trying to leave?" Gabe asked as he closed the hood of the Buick.

"We need to be leaving like now!" Brianna told him. "We driving out to Boca Raton, and I wanna stop and pick up a few things from the store."

Gabe nodded his head and looked over at Duke. He told him to holla at Boo Man to see if the fat boy wanted to roll with them. He then followed alongside Brianna as the two of them headed toward the elevator.

* * *

Half an hour later, they drove away from the penthouse in Brianna's Benz truck, with Duke and Boo Man in the back seat. Lorenzo and his girl, Rachell, rode with Sherry and Tamara in her

Land Rover Range Rover behind the Benz. Gabe made a stop at a Walmart at Brianna's request so she could grab a few things for the reunion.

They hit the road after leaving the Walmart and took I-95. Gabe's Benz was filled with Mint Condition's "Believe in Us" as he and Brianna shared a blunt while Duke and Boo Man passed a blunt back and forth between the two of them.

Once they reached Boca Raton and turned down the street, into what could only be described as a rich neighborhood, Gabe slowed the truck in front of the tall, black steel gate that had two suit-wearing men at the entrance. He pulled to a stop as Brianna leaned over to the driver's side as Gabe let down the window.

Gabe listened as Brianna spoke with the two armed security guards, and he then pulled the truck through the opened gate. He parked the Benz inside the open area to which Brianna had pointed, alongside a crowd of other cars. They all got out and made their way toward the walkway that led to the custom-built, one-story estate.

"Yo, Brianna!" Duke called out to her as he and the rest of the crew walked up the long walkway toward the mansion.

"What's up, Duke?" Brianna answered as they passed the golden statues of two lions and a water fountain that sat dead center in the walkway.

"I just wanna know!" Duke started. "Yo' mom's rich or something? I mean, look at this house she's living in!"

"Actually!" Brianna stated as she stopped at the front door to the mansion and turned to face Duke. "Because you my man's homeboy, I'll tell you this. It's not my mom who's rich, but my step-father that's with all the money."

"So you mean—?"

Duke was cut off when they heard the mansion doors begin to open. Brianna broke into a smile when she saw her mother and step-father standing in the doorway. She rushed over to both of them, first hugging her mother and then her step-father, Darrell.

"Ummm, excuse me!" Victoria Murphy said as she stood with her hands on her hips staring at Lorenzo, Sherry, Tamara, and Rachell. "I know the four of you ain't just going to stand there. Y'all better get over here and give me a hug!"

Brianna smiled as Lorenzo and her girls all crowded her mother, all hugging her at once. She looked over to Gabe standing alongside Duke and Boo Man. Brianna then released her step-father and walked over to Gabe. She took his hand in hers as she then led him over to stand in front of her parents.

"Momma, Darrell," Brianna stated, getting their attention, "I want you two to meet—!"

"Is this the young man Gabriel, who Erica told us about?" Darrell spoke up asking his step-daughter, while taking in the young man who stood beside her. "So, young man, you're seeing my daughter?"

Gabe stepped forward and held out his hand to the tall, slightly muscular, dark-brown-skinned, clean-shaven, bald-headed middle-aged man with a sharp-edge goatee that was salt-and-pepper. Gabe first shook hands with Brianna's father and then with her mother.

"Yes, sir. I've only been seeing Brianna for a short time, but please understand that neither you nor Mrs.—!"

"Murphy!" Victoria finished for the amazingly handsome young man.

Gabe smiled at Brianna's mother at her help, and then continued what he was saying to Darrell.

"Neither you nor Mrs. Murphy need worry. I give you my word that Brianna is in good hands."

"Good hands, you say?" Darrell stated with a small smile appearing on his lips. He then nodded and continued. "We'll talk more, young man.

We'll talk more later."

* * *

Brianna became separated from Gabe and Lorenzo after her mother dragged her, Rachell, Sherry, and Tamara out to the back patio that was built for entertaining. She noticed that most of the females in her family were all crowded out by the pool. When she glanced back, she saw Darrell leading both her man and Lorenzo up the stairs that led onto the wide balcony area with furniture where the men were entertained.

As Brianna received hugs from her aunts, cousins, and grandmothers, she caught a few questions concerning her new man from some of her relatives and even her mother's mother. She then spotted Erica, Ebony, and Brittany seated and talking by the pool.

"I see you ain't wasting time running your mouth about Gabriel," Brianna said as she walked up on her sister and her friends.

Erica recognized her sister's voice and turned around to see Brianna walking up behind her.

"Don't sound so embarrassed! You're the one that decided to mess with a young high school boy instead of someone your own age!"

"You know, Erica, it's really easy to tell when you're upset or worried, because your eyes give you away, just like now. Your eyes are showing that you're jealous that some young boy chose me, when it was you that wanted him. Get over it, big Sis!" Brianna said with a small smile.

Brianna walked off and left Erica staring angrily at her, only to realize that she was jealous. However, Erica was always the one who was spoiled and given whatever she wanted, while Brianna was left to work for everything she ever received. Brianna then shifted her eyes up to the balcony and smiled at the sight of her man and step-father talking and laughing together.

* * *

Brianna kept a close eye on her man throughout the family reunion, finally getting him back after everyone had eaten and was just relaxing and listening to music by Vivian Green. The song "Anything Out There" was playing on the system Darrell had set up throughout the house and could be heard clearly on the back patio and in the pool area. Brianna was sitting on top of Gabe's lap talking with a few members of her family when her step-father appeared.

"Baby girl!" Darrell said, getting her attention. "Can I get you away from my boy Gabriel for just a few minutes?"

Brianna's kiss to Gabe made her cousins

giggle at the sight. She got up from her man's lap and started to follow alongside Darrell until the both of them were inside the house and seated at the bar.

"So, what's up, Darrell?" Brianna asked as the bartender set down a drink in front of each of them.

Darrell nodded his thanks to Tim, took a sip from his glass, and then looked over at his step-daughter.

"I've spoken with the young man Gabriel. I can truthfully say that he is a very impressive young man, even though he only just turned eighteen yesterday."

"Darrell, he may be—!"

Darrell held up his hand and cut off Brianna before she could start explaining anything further.

"I've also spoken with your friend Lorenzo concerning this Gabriel, and I've come to understand that the young man is very useful with . . . let's just put it this way, Brianna: our Gabriel has no problems with putting down problems, just as he did last night!" Darrell continued.

"Lorenzo told you that?" Brianna asked her step-father.

"Actually, it was Gabriel that told me about last night!"

"Wait!" Brianna interrupted Darrell. "Gabriel told you about last night?"

Darrell disregarded Brianna's question and said, "Do you think you're able to get our young Gabriel to come to work for us?"

"I've tried to get him to work with me selling the pills."

"You misunderstood, Brianna!" Darrell told her. "I'm not speaking about him selling anything for us. I'm speaking of his dealing with the problems that we've discussed with the others."

"You mean . . . ?" Brianna started as she sat staring at her step-father with a look that expressed more than just her feelings toward what Darrell was asking. "Darrell, I'm sorry, but Gabriel isn't some type of hit man!"

"I'm willing to offer him $50,000 for the normal problems and $125,000 for our more major problems."

"Darrell, I'm telling you again! Gabriel isn't a hit man!"

"Am I interrupting?"

Brianna heard Gabe's smooth and perfectly deep voice. She then looked past Darrell to see her man standing at the opening of the patio door with his hands in his pockets. She stood from her stool as Gabe walked over. She stared at his facial expression and was really unable to read anything from his calm and normal expression.

"I won't act like I didn't hear a little of what was being said about me," Gabe told both Brianna and Darrell. "I heard the numbers, but I didn't hear what the numbers were for!"

"Babe, it's nothing!" Brianna spoke up, only for Darrell to interrupt.

"I was just telling Brianna that I may have a job for you."

"Darrell, he's not—!"

"Bri!" Gabe stated, shifting his eyes over to meet hers. "I wanna hear what Darrell is offering."

Brianna wanted to argue, but she just sighed loudly as she picked up her drink. She kissed Gabe on the lips before dismissing herself and exiting back outside onto the back patio with the rest of the family.

G abe and Brianna left her parents' house and returned to Miami after 10:00 p.m. and was back at her penthouse by 11:15 p.m. They made the trip home in complete silence, even with Duke and Boo Man in the back seat. Gabe had a lot of shit on his mind after talking to Brianna's step-father about his offer to basically become his paid hit man. Brianna remained quiet since she was upset with Darrell for disregarding what she had to say, and she was also upset with Gabe since he still had yet to tell her what he and Darrell talked about and decided upon.

After the others had left and Brianna and Gabe were inside the penthouse, she headed straight to their bedroom, stripped, and got ready for a shower. She was just climbing into the Jacuzzi bathtub, after filling it with water and scented bath wash, when she looked up and saw Gabe enter the bathroom in nothing but a pair of Polo boxers that she bought for him.

Brianna relaxed in the hot water as she watched Gabe step out of his boxers. She lowered her eyes from his muscular and defined chest that was tattooed from the right side to half of his right arm and elbow. She then dropped her eyes to his flaccid dick that was still fat, thick, and long.

Once Gabe was inside the tub with her and slid in behind her, Brianna got comfortable between Gabe's legs, leaned back against his chest, and sighed softly as he wrapped his arms around her.

"You still mad at me, ma?" Gabe whispered into her ear, kissing her neck afterward.

Although Brianna heard his question, she didn't bother with an answer.

"So, are you going to tell me about the talk with Darrell? Did you accept his offer, Gabriel?"

"Do you trust me?"

"What?"

"I said, do you trust me, Bri?" he asked again as he stared into her eyes as she stared back at him over her shoulder.

"Gabriel, what does that have to do with what I just asked you?"

"Because, if you trust me, you trust me to handle my business each day I have to and be back home with you as I'm supposed to. So, again, do you trust me, ma?"

Brianna stared at Gabe a few moments before she began shaking her head after getting her answer to her question. Brianna then stood up from between his legs and climbed out from the tub. On the way out of the bathroom, she grabbed a towel from the rack and left Gabe alone inside the tub.

* * *

Gabe made it into the bedroom a little while after Brianna left the bathroom, only to find her in the bed and facing away from him. Gabe climbed into bed with her under the blanket, but he slid over behind his woman.

"Move, Gabriel!" Brianna told him, only for Gabe to ignore her and roll her over onto her back.

He then climbed on top of her and positioned himself between her legs. She was fully aware that he was still fully naked. Gabe watched Brianna's eyes as he removed her panties and then helped her out of the wifebeater she was wearing. He then noticed she wasn't refusing him, and when he bent down and kissed her lips, she instantly responded.

"Mmmmmm, Gabriel!" Brianna broke the kiss by moaning as she felt her man sliding slowly into her.

She wrapped her arms around his neck as he slid in and out of her, pushing deeper each time.

"I need you to trust me, ma!" Brianna heard her man whisper into her ear as he slowly deep-stroked her just right.

"I do, babe! I trust your ass, Gabriel!" she cried out.

18

A week after the family reunion with Brianna's family and the agreement with her step-father, Gabe continued with his normal living. He even went on another job with Duke. But he now added Boo Man since he found out that Silk and Shantae were chilling back from making any moves. He had Simon once again put down his computer skills and help him and his crew rob another big-time jeweler. This time, Duke had been watching the home of the jeweler, and he knew that the man brought home a black briefcase every night that was filled with diamonds and gold.

Boo Man and Duke were already inside when they caught the jeweler once he walked through his front door. They attacked the man and his armed escort, and forced them both facedown to the floor at gunpoint.

"We can make this simple or we can make this bloody!" Gabe spoke up, once both the jeweler and his escort were facedown.

Gabe walked over to the man, squatted down beside him, and laid the burner across his back.

"I prefer simple, but my friends like things

bloody!"

"Sss-simple!" the business man got out in a shaky voice.

"Smart man!" Gabe said with a smile behind his ski mask as he put the man on his back with the hammer.

Eight minutes after getting everything that was inside the bedroom and office safes, Gabe, Duke, and Boo Man rushed from the mansion with two full backpacks and a briefcase. They then jumped into the stolen 2013 Lexus G3 350 and took off.

After getting away with the hit on the jewelry store owner, Gabe then hooked up with Paul Lewis and initially received a little more than $70,000. Then Gabe produced three pouches filled with over twenty-five small diamonds in each bag. He and Paul sat for more than four hours before coming to an agreement that Gabe would receive $25 million per pouch, for a total of $75 million. The two of them then discussed payment since Paul first had to get the money to pay Gabe. He told him that it would take him two or three days, at the most.

Gabe explained to Boo Man and Duke about the agreement with Paul Lewis. He then kept things real with his boy Simon and explained about wanting to split the money four ways, since Simon was the reason they were even able to get to the jeweler so easily. Gabe made sure it was also understood that everyone was to act the same way once they received the money. He didn't want any unwanted attention drawn to them.

Gabe heard about the robbery on the news later that night. The jeweler's wife had returned home and found her husband and his security escort completely naked and hog-tied in the middle of the living room. Gabe lay in his bed watching the news report with Brianna beside him, with her head against his chest. He waited until the report was over, and then he turned the television off.

"So that's your work, isn't it?" Brianna chimed in.

Gabe looked down at Brianna after she lifted her head from his chest, only to rest her chin back onto his chest and stare at him. He saw no anger in her eyes, so he gave her a simple nod of the head. He then broke down everything that was happening with the jewelry, gold, and diamonds.

"So you're making back less than what they said the diamonds were worth?" Brianna asked him. "You said $75 million for all three pouches, right?"

"Pretty much!"

Brianna nodded and then laid her head back down onto her man's chest. After a moment she spoke up again.

"I owe you a birthday party since we never went to the club on your birthday."

"It's cool, Bri!"

"I want you in school tomorrow. You haven't been to school this whole week, Gabriel. I know you're handling your business, but I don't want no dumb dude—and, no, I'm not calling you dumb, babe. I just want you to understand how important finishing school is. You understand what I'm saying, Gabriel?"

"Ma, all you had to say was go to school, and I was gone!" Gabe told her, causing Brianna to smile as she lifted her head and looked back at him.

She then climbed on top of him and straddled her man as she began pushing up his wifebeater. Brianna slowly grinded on his print and felt his dick begin to swell under her. A smile soon appeared on her lips as she stared down into her man's gorgeous eyes.

* * *

Gabe was up early the next morning and got in a good twenty-minute workout in the gym Brianna had begun setting up in the penthouse. He took a shower afterward, and once he was finished, he walked back into the bedroom to find Brianna gone.

He got dressed in one of the Gucci outfits Brianna had picked out for him, along with a Gucci fitted hat that went with the outfit. He was putting on his all-white Air Force Ones, just as Brianna stepped back into the bedroom.

"Hey, handsome!" Brianna said as she walked up behind Gabe and wrapped her arms around him from the back. She kissed his neck and smelled his cologne.

"What's up, ma?" Gabe replied as he slid his money, keys, and cell phone into his pocket, before he turned to face Brianna and kiss her on the lips.

"Eddie's feeding Duchess, and your food is waiting for you," Brianna told him once the kiss ended.

She looked her man over and smiled at how good he looked. She could actually feel that she was getting wet between her legs just by the sight of him.

After heading downstairs, Brianna and Gabe discussed meeting up during his lunch break. Gabe then broke out in a smile when he heard Duchess come rushing toward him and barking the whole way.

Brianna smiled as she stood watching Gabe with his dog and seeing how much Duchess was in love with her man. She had to laugh at the simple fact that she could actually understand Duchess's love for Gabriel Green.

While Gabe and Brianna ate breakfast, Duchess sat inside her lap eating from her hand. Brianna told Gabe everything she had to do that day. After finishing his meal, Gabe kissed Brianna on the lips and then headed for the front door.

As he took the elevator down to the garage, Gabe dug out his cell phone and hit up his boy, Duke.

"Yo!" Duke answered at the start of the second ring.

* * *

Duke hung up with his boy Gabe and was all smiles as he walked back over to where Melody, Boo Man, Gina, Shantae, and Kiki were standing.

He slid his phone back into his pocket as he stopped beside Melody.

"What's so funny?" Melody asked after looking up at Duke and seeing a big grin on his face. "Who was that on the phone?"

"That was Gabe's ass!" Duke replied, still smiling, only to look at his sister and hear her suck her teeth and roll her eyes. He turned back to Melody and said, "His crazy ass just called me talking crazy!"

"What's my dude talking about?" Boo Man asked.

Duke shook his head again and answered Melody's question.

"He's talking about getting engaged."

"What?" both Melody and Shantae yelled in unison.

"Duke, you playing, right?" Melody screamed.

Duke was still smiling when he shook his head no.

"That's what my nigga just told me!"

"Who the fuck is he marrying?" Shantae asked nastily. "He marrying that new bitch he's messing with?"

"Duke, what is Shantae talking about?"

Melody asked, turning to face her boyfriend.

Duke sighed loudly already preparing for the bullshit. Just as he was about to open his mouth and explain, he paused when he heard DMX and Sisqó's "What These Bitches Want" banging from somebody's sound system. He looked out at the street and saw Gabe's Chevy Caprice drop-top sitting on twenty-six-inch Asantis and Lionhart tires.

"Naw!" Boo Man said, smiling as he also stood staring at the Donk with Gabe behind the wheel. "This dude just don't stop, do he? Where the fuck he get the Caprice from?"

"Duke!" Gina cried, smiling as she watched Gabe pull into the parking lot. "Isn't that the old car my mom gave him?"

"Yeah!" Duke said as he started walking toward the Donk as Gabe pulled up and stopped the car. "What's up, my nigga?"

"What's good, playboy?" Gabe said, dapping up with Duke as Boo Man, Melody, and Gina all walked up to the Caprice.

"Gabe, this my momma's car?" Gina asked as she looked inside and saw the seashell color interior and full fiberglass dashboard, doors, and console. She also noticed the digital gauges, the twenty-three-inch LED TV, and the twelve-inch LCD monitor. "You really fixed this thing up, Gabe! I like it!"

"Gabe, I wanna know what this is I'm hearing about you getting engaged, boy," Melody said as she stood with her hands on her hips while staring at him.

Gabe cut his eyes over at Duke and watched his boy smirking and looking off in another direction.

"I'm just thinking about it, Melody. But if I do decide on it, it's just an engagement, ma. I'm not getting married anytime soon!" Gabe looked back and said to Melody.

"Who is she?" Melody asked him, before she pointed at Shantae. "What about you and Shantae? I thought you two was together?"

Gabe looked over at Shantae and saw her staring hard back at him. He held her eyes until she rolled hers, and then both she and Kiki walked off.

"I'ma let you holla at Shantae about us, or what was us!" Gabe said as he looked back at Melody.

* * *

Shantae was unable to believe the shit she

heard about Gabe and whoever the bitch was he was supposedly dealing with now. She sat inside her first class feeling herself getting more and more upset. She was really getting upset over the idea that her man was now with his next bitch, when they hadn't even broken up.

Shantae left her fourth-period class early and waited outside of Gabe's fourth-period class until the bell went off and the students began leaving the room.

"Gabe!"

He heard his name as he was talking with a female with whom he was walking out of the classroom. He looked to his right and over his shoulder, just as Shantae walked up to him.

"What are you doing out here, Shantae?"

"We need to talk, Gabe!" she told him.

"Naw!" Gabe replied. "We really don't!"

"Gabe!" Shantae yelled as he walked off.

She rushed behind him and grabbed his arm as he was walking out through the exit to the staircase.

"We need to talk! How you just gonna get with the next bitch when we never broke up?" Shantae asked.

"You serious, ain't you?" Gabe asked, while

staring at Shantae like she was insane. He continued as he turned to face her. "Shantae, shit was over between us once you decided your loyalty was to the same dude that was beating ya ass, and said fuck me!"

"Gabe, I never said fuck you!" Shantae told him, grabbing his arm again and stopping him from walking away. "You're my man, but now you messing with the next bitch and talking about getting engaged and shit! What type of time is you on, nigga?"

"A'ight, ma! Tell me something real quick! Since this nigga Silk has been in the hospital, you been to see him yet?" Gabe said, lightly laughing.

"No!" Shantae lied, wanting to prove to Gabe that she wanted only him.

Gabe shook his head as he stood staring at her.

"Yeah! You made your decision, Shantae, and you just ensured it by lying. I know you went to see the nigga the same day he went in the hospital. And you've gone three more times since dude's been home!"

Shantae was caught off guard by what Gabe just told her. She stood watching Gabe walk down the stairs, but then called out to him as she rushed behind her man.

* * *

"Where's my babe at, Duke?" Brianna asked after climbing from her truck.

She stood in front of the Benz with Duke and Boo Man, after they noticed her and walked over.

"He should be out here in a few minutes!" Duke replied, just as he heard his name and looked behind him.

"Here comes Melody, fam!" Boo Man stated as he saw Melody heading their way.

"That's your woman, Duke?" Brianna asked, smiling as she watched the young girl coming her way.

"Yeah!" Duke answered, when he noticed the look on Melody's face.

"Ummm, what's going on, Derrick Mitchell?" Melody asked, using Duke's government name. "I was looking for you, and you're out here with her! Who is she?"

"Relax, Melody!" Boo Man spoke up. But he just as quickly shut up when Melody shot him a look.

"Baby, this is Brianna!" Duke told her. "She's Gabe's girlfriend."

"You're the one he wants to marry?" Melody got out, just before Duke covered her mouth with both his hands.

"What did she say, Duke?" Brianna asked, staring first at Duke's girlfriend and then over to him.

"Noth—!"

Duke heard someone yelling Gabe's name. Immediately, he, Melody, Boo Man, and Brianna all stared back into the parking lot to see Gabe walking quickly with Shantae rushing up behind him. Shantae grabbed his arm and snatched him around, and then kissed him directly on his lips.

"Oh hell no!" Brianna said while staring at the young bitch who was all over Gabe; and before she knew it, she was already headed toward her man.

"Oh shit!" Boo Man said, just as he and Duke took off after Brianna.

* * *

Gabe was caught off guard after Shantae kissed him and was now wrapped around his neck and hugging him. Gabe got control of himself and was just beginning to pull her away when he was jerked hard by Brianna.

"Bitch! I don't know who—!"

Gabe recognized Brianna's voice and wondered where the hell she came from. He rushed and got in between the two young women, just in time to see Shantae reach for her straight razor that she always kept between her breasts inside her bra.

"Enough!" Gabe yelled, causing not only Brianna and Shantae to pause at staring at him, but also everybody else who was close by and watching.

"Gabe!" Duke called as he, Boo Man, and Melody rushed up. "My nigga, you good?"

Gabe ignored his boy and focused back on Shantae.

"Shantae, this my last time saying this shit! You made your decision. I'm done!"

"Gabe!" Shantae yelled, even as he turned to the female that ran up on her.

Gabe ignored Shantae as he grabbed Brianna's hand and pulled her behind him, leading her out to her truck that he saw parked in the middle of the damn street.

19

Brianna was pissed off and just stared out the window of her own damn truck as her supposed man drove away from his high school after the bullshit that just went down. She swung her head around to look at Gabe, noticing that his ass was extra quiet all of a sudden.

She then turned toward his ass and said, "Oh, so you ain't got shit to say now, right? What the fuck was that shit, Gabriel?"

Gabe turned his head and looked over at Brianna and saw her face all balled up.

"It was nothing, Brianna," he calmly said as he focused back on the road.

"What?" she yelled at Gabe. "Nigga, what the fuck you mean it was nothing? So the next bitch kissing you ain't nothing, right? Remember that shit, so when I see me a fine-ass dude, I'ma tongue his ass down too!"

"I hope you plan on paying for that same nigga's funeral, because I promise I'ma body that fool as soon as you try me, Brianna!" Gabe yelled, cutting his eyes back over to her. "Don't test me, Brianna! I'm not the one to test, ma!"

"Oh, but I'm the—!"

"I told you it was nothing!" Gabe barked at Brianna. He then got under control and in a calmer voice said, "I asked you before if you trust me. Don't change your mind now, because I haven't given you a reason not to."

Brianna sucked her teeth and rolled her eyes as she turned her attention back out the window. She said nothing else to Gabe until he pulled up in front of an apartment complex out in Hollywood a little while later.

"What the hell are we doing here, Gabe? I'm hungry!"

"I need to pick up something real quick!" Gabe told her as he was parking the truck.

Brianna sighed loudly as Gabe climbed his ass out of the truck. He ignored her when he shut the driver's door and walked into the complex. She wanted to scream at him for how he was ignoring her. She then heard her phone begin to ring, so she dug it out of her Gucci purse and saw that Sherry was on the other line.

"What, Sherry?"

"Brianna, where you at?"

"I'm with Gabriel's ass out here in Hollywood. Why?"

"We may have a problem out here in the city

with those same dudes that robbed the young dude Jit Jit you put on!"

"What happened now?"

"Jit Jit just called me talking about them same dudes out in front of the apartment who are trying to fuck with him and the customers."

Brianna saw Gabe walking back to the truck carrying some type of pouch, and she told Sherry she was on her way. She then hung up the phone just as Gabe climbed back inside.

"Here!" Gabe said as he tossed the black leather pouch over onto Brianna's lap. "Hold on to that until we get where we're going!"

"Gabe, we need to drive out to Liberty City!" Brianna told him while she was unzipping the pouch.

"What's out in Liberty City?" Gabe asked.

"Gabriel, where'd you get all this money from?"

"It's mine!" he answered, but then asked again, "What's out in the city, Brianna?"

"I need to deal with a problem!" she told Gabe as she zipped back up the pouch filled with money.

* * *

Sherry watched as Brianna's Benz truck

J. L. ROSE

pulling into the complex. She, Tamara, Lorenzo, and Jit Jit were standing on the second level of the apartment from which Jit Jit sold pills and weed for Brianna. Sherry pointed out the truck to the others, and then she started toward the stairs with the others right behind her.

"I see she brought my dude with her!" Lorenzo stated, smiling at the sight of Gabe climbing from behind the wheel of the Benz truck.

"Who's the pretty boy with Brianna?" Jit Jit asked as he hard-stared at the dude walking with his woman.

"Relax, lil gangsta!" Tamara said, smiling after noticing Jit Jit's facial expression and knowing about his feelings for Brianna. "That's Brianna's man, but don't let his good looks fool you!"

"Listen to her, lil homie!" Lorenzo told Jit Jit, just as both Brianna and Gabe walked up.

"What's going on now, Jit Jit?" Brianna asked her young hustler.

"It's this clown-ass nigga Show Time again!" Jit Jit told her as he couldn't help noticing the pretty muthafucker that stood beside his woman. "If you would have let me deal with the nigga after we got robbed the first time, we wouldn't be dealing with 'im now!"

"Where's he at now, Jit Jit?" Brianna asked, ignoring his attitude.

"I don't even much know where the fuck nigga went at, Brianna! It's him and four other dudes, but they just left a few minutes ago!"

"Here they come now!" Tamara called out, seeing the Impala that was slowly creeping up the street in their direction.

Brianna looked around behind her and saw the Impala had parked a short distance from her Benz truck. She then spotted Show Time as soon as his ass climbed from the car and broke out in a smile once he noticed her.

Brianna heard Gabe mumble something, and she looked back at him as he was sliding something inside the back of his jeans and out of her sight. Brianna met his eyes only to see him look past her.

"It's about time you finally showed up!" a voice said.

Brianna turned back around to face Show Time and his boys. She looked him over in disgust.

"What the fuck is the problem, Show Time? I

thought we had an understanding."

"We did!" Show Time started. "But now I'ma need more, or we both know how this shit gonna play out!"

"Lorenzo!" Brianna called when she saw him reach for his waist to the right of her.

She saw the look on his face but shook her head at him, and then focused back on Show Time.

"Show Time, you're wasting your time! We had an understanding, and if you can't continue as things were, then we have nothing left to discuss!"

"So that's how you feel, huh?" Show Time asked as he took a step closer to Brianna, before he froze in mid-step once a chrome .40 caliber appeared in front of his face.

"You may wanna reverse that foot, playboy!" Gabe spoke up as he held the .40 aimed at Show Time.

Gabe ignored the other dudes who were watching but had their hands at their waist but weren't pulling, only staring.

"I won't repeat what was just said, because you heard just like everybody else. Decide now!"

"Yo, Brianna!" Show Time called out. "Who

the fuck is this dude?"

"That's not an answer, playboy!" Gabe told him as he stepped toward Show Time and began patting him down.

He found a 9mm and a nice-sized knot of cash that he tossed back over to Jit Jit.

"So since you can't decide, I'ma decide for you! It's over, playboy! Whatever deal you had with Brianna is over, and this better be the last time you're seen over here! We understand each other? Nod ya head if you understand!"

Brianna smiled as she stood watching Show Time nodding his head in understanding. She held back from laughing out loud when Gabe told Show Time and his boys to strip and get completely naked—ass naked.

* * *

Shantae looked for Gabe after lunch break and then again after school, but she never found his ass anywhere. She saw his Chevy Caprice still parked in the same spot, so she decided to wait in the student parking lot until he showed up. She and her girl Kiki sat listening to music and even made a trip out to the store, and the Caprice was still there when they returned.

"Shantae, why don't you just call this boy?"

Kiki asked as she and Shantae sat smoking a blunt that Shantae had rolled up from the weed she had inside her purse.

"Girl, he's not gonna answer!" Shantae told Kiki as she passed her a blunt. "He's like that when he's mad, and if he still with—!"

"Who this?" Kiki asked, interrupting Shantae after seeing a Land Rover turning inside the parking lot.

Shantae climbed out from her Mustang and stared at the Land Rover Range Rover as a brown-skinned woman stepped out from the passenger side and then started walking toward Gabe's car.

"Ummm, excuse me!"

Sherry looked to her right after hearing another voice and saw a female who she recognized from the last time she was at the school for Gabe's birthday. She then turned to face Shantae.

"Yeah!"

"Who are you?" Shantae asked as she walked over to Sherry. "Where's Gabe?"

"Look," Sherry stated as she softly sighed, "I'm just here to pick up Gabe's car. But if you want him, I think you should call him."

"So you telling me you don't—!"

"Sherry!" Tamara called from inside the Land Rover Range Rover. "Girl, let's go! We still gotta handle this other shit before the party."

Shantae watched as the girl she now knew as Sherry climbed inside Gabe's car. A few moments later, the Chevy Caprice was trailing the Land Rover Range Rover out of the parking lot.

20

Lorenzo stepped back outside for the fifth time, not surprised at the crowd that was in front of Club Paradise. He ignored the crowd and the yelling as he stood looking around to see if Brianna and Gabe had finally shown up yet. He dug out his cell phone after not seeing either of their trucks in the parking lot. He was just about to dial Brianna's number, when someone grabbed his arm.

"Lorenzo!" Sherry yelled as she walked up beside him. "Brianna just called. They coming up the street now!"

Lorenzo slid his phone back into his pocket and looked toward the entrance as a crowd of cars and two SUVs pulled up in front of the club. He was just about to turn away after not recognizing any of the vehicles, but he paused when he heard the bass of Beanie Sigel's "It's On" fearing Jay-Z.

"No this boy didn't!" Sherry exclaimed as a huge smile grew on her face as the diamond black and chrome '75 Buick LeSabre slowly pulled up and stopped in front of the club.

She and Lorenzo stood watching as Gabe got

out of the Buick, walked around to the passenger side, and opened the car door to allow Brianna to climb out as well.

"Well, damn, youngin'!" Lorenzo said, smiling as he looked Gabe over in the silk white and gray metallic pinstripe suit with matching suede Kenneth Coles on his feet. "I see you, young homie! You doing ya thing, youngin'!"

"Both they asses look good!" Sherry said, seeing the form-fitting skirt that matched Gabe's suit, along with a floor-length white leather jacket that Brianna was wearing. "You two are really showing out tonight out here!"

"It's my baby's birthday even if it's late!" Brianna said, smiling over at Gabe as she wrapped her left hand around his arm and leaned in against him.

"Well, now that you two finally—!"

"Hold the hell up!" Sherry yelled, cutting off Lorenzo as Gabe and Brianna stared at her like she was crazy.

Sherry ignored their stares as she grabbed Brianna's hand from Gabe's arm. She held it up so she was able to see the square-cut pink diamond ring with a platinum band.

"What is this shit, Brianna?"

Brianna broke out in a huge smile as she looked from Sherry over to Gabe, who stood with a smirk on his lips. Brianna looked back to her girl and said, "It's from my fiancé!"

"Your what?" Sherry cried, looking to a just-as-surprised Lorenzo and then back to Brianna, who still stood with a smile. "Oh my God! Are you serious?"

Brianna nodded her head yes even after Sherry grabbed her in a hug and screamed out loud, causing a scene. Brianna then looked over to her fiancé and saw him and Lorenzo embracing each other in a brotherly hug.

* * *

Brianna and Sherry entered the club to Jay-Z and Beyoncé's "Bonnie and Clyde" banging from the club's speakers, which caused them to scream and throw their hands up in the air. They began to shake their bodies to the music as both Lorenzo and Gabe stood smiling and watching them.

Once the girls got over their little moment, the four of them finally made it into the VIP section. Two muscular and tall security men blocked the stairwell, but they moved when Sherry stepped up, and she then led the others upstairs. She stepped in first, followed by Lorenzo, Brianna, and then Gabe in the back.

"Happy birthday!"

Gabe smiled his normal smirk as he stood with Brianna looking at the packed VIP area, and saw friends and people who he didn't know. He walked into the crowd and was surrounded by people who Brianna began introducing to him as friends and members of her team. He then spotted Duke, Boo Man, Melody, and Gina, and was even happier when he saw Nicole appear in front of him with a big smile on her face.

"Happy belated birthday, sweetheart!" Nicole told her step-son as she hugged his neck tightly while he returned the hug.

After Gabe released Nicole, who was on his left with Brianna on his right, he looked up to see Erica approaching him. He was caught off guard after seeing how she was dressed in a short dress that hugged her body and perky breasts so tight that he could see her every curve. He also could see that she wasn't wearing a bra since her phat nipples were clearly showing through her top.

"Hi, handsome!" Erica said, smiling as she stopped in front of Gabe.

She watched the expression on his face as she slid into his arms and hugged him, making sure to press her body in against his. She kissed him on the cheek and then slowly released him and met his eyes.

"So, how does it feel, gorgeous? I mean, to be eighteen now?"

Gabe caught on to exactly what Erica really meant, and he saw the mischievous smile she had on her lips. He was about to open his mouth in response, only for Brianna to speak up first.

"Oh trust, Gabe knows what it's like to be eighteen, since he's all man in more ways than one!"

"Anyway!" Erica said with a smile, after seeing that she had Brianna showing her jealousy. She then turned around and handed Gabe his present. "This is for you, handsome! Happy birthday, babe . . . I mean Gabe!"

Gabe spoke up quickly after catching Erica's slipup and seeing Brianna about to act a fool. He then thanked Erica for the gift, and then led both Nicole and a pissed-off Brianna over to the table where Lorenzo and the others were waiting.

"This bitch is really trying my mutha—!"

Gabe interrupted Brianna before she got started and caused a scene at the table among their friends. He kissed her on the lips, which shut her up, and within moments, her arms were wrapped around his neck and they were locked in a passionate kiss until Gabe broke it.

Brianna opened her eyes after a moment and smiled.

"What was that for?" she asked.

"To shut you up!" Lorenzo answered, causing the table to burst out laughing.

After the laughter died down, Sherry quickly spoke up and got everyone's attention in the VIP section.

"I need everybody to focus on both my girl Brianna and my boo Gabe. They have an announcement to make."

Brianna gave Sherry a look and shook her head, and then she looked over at Gabe, who sat smiling and watching her.

"You wanna tell 'em, or you want me to tell 'em?"

"I'll tell 'em!" Sherry yelled out as she excitedly announced that Gabe and Brianna were engaged to be married.

* * *

Erica was unable to believe what she had just heard, even though she sat just a few feet away from her sister and Gabe. Brianna then showed off the diamond ring Gabe had given to her for their engagement. Erica stared hatefully at Brianna as the bitch sat smiling and lying all under Gabe. Erica then snatched up her purse and stood from her seat. She left the VIP section, since she didn't want to be around her so-called sister anymore.

Erica dug out her cell phone as she was heading down the stairs. She was so caught up in making a quick text message that she slammed straight into somebody, dropping both her phone and her purse.

"My fault!" the person said as he went down into a squat to help the female pick up her things from the ground.

"It's my fault! I wasn't watching where I—!"

"Erica?"

Erica was surprised when she looked up and realized who she was looking at.

"Anthony, what are you doing here?"

"I was just about to ask you the same question!" Anthony replied as he and Erica stood back up. "I thought you weren't into going out to clubs."

Erica caught the way Anthony was looking her over.

"I'm only here because of Brianna's fiancé's birthday party!" she replied.

"Wait!" Anthony stated, unsure he heard her correctly. "You say whose birthday party, Erica?"

Erica's face balled up, but she slowly let out a sneaky smile as an idea came to her.

"Anthony, who you here with, boo?"

* * *

Darrell Murphy climbed from the back of the Maybach G4 once the car stopped out in front of the night club and the armed chauffeur opened the door. He was met by a team of his security. He then turned to help out his wife, who stood watching two of their closest and most trusted friends and business associates.

"I really can't believe I let you talk me into coming to this place!" George Warren told Darrell as they were escorted from the Maybach into the club.

"Don't start complaining, Warren!" Trinity Sullivan told George, shooting him a look that caused Victoria to laugh and shake her head at the both of them.

They always argued every time the two of them got around each other.

"George, just trust me, old friend!" Darrell

told him as the four of them were escorted through the crowded club.

"This kid just may be what we've been waiting on, George!"

"I'm only doing this because—!"

George paused in the middle of his conversation at the commotion that was taking place just a few feet away from him. He stood up with the others and watched as a young man stumbled down the stairs from the VIP section. A second young man calmly made his way downstairs followed by the rest of his crew in the VIP section.

"Darrell!" Victoria cried out, recognizing both young men and seeing both her daughters in the crowd.

Darrell heard his wife but watched the young man who was seeing his step-daughter doing a number on the other young man, who he remembered used to see his step-daughter. George smiled at the combination that Gabe threw at Anthony, which sent the boy back down to the ground.

"Darrell!"

Darrell heard the tone in which his wife had called his name, so he looked at her and saw her pointing. Darrell saw the team of club security men rushing through the crowd to get to where the problem was taking place.

* * *

Gabe stopped and stared down at the guy he now knew was Brianna's ex-boyfriend, Anthony. Anthony was now disoriented and bleeding badly from the nose, his mouth, and under his left eye. Gabe shook his head and was looking back at Brianna just as he was grabbed by security.

Reacting on impulse, Gabe snatched his left arm away while turning toward his right side. He squatted low as he swung a solid right hook that slammed into the mid-section of the person that had grabbed him. Gabe followed with a left uppercut that knocked homeboy back into the crowd behind him.

* * *

"Jesus!" George said, smiling after seeing how hard the young man hit the club security right before a few of Darrell's men rushed over to stop the fight.

"He has amazing strength, and he's swift with both his feet and hands!" Trinity stated, impressed with the display she had just witnessed.

"I'm glad you two approve of the young man

you are both watching!" Darrell told Trinity and George with a wide smile. "That is the same young man the two of you are here to meet tonight!"

Darrell noticed the surprised but pleased looks on both his friends' faces after witnessing firsthand what Gabe was capable of. He motioned them both to follow behind him as he took his wife's hand and began walking toward the crowd. He then noticed the club owner appear from out of the crowd with two suit-wearing men that were most likely his bodyguards.

21

B rianna dealt with the owner of the night club and apologized for the trouble. They came to an understanding with some type of payment for the problem. Brianna then led her fiancé back up into the VIP section and wasn't surprised to see her mother and Darrell seated at her table with their friends. She nodded her head in thanks to Lorenzo as he brought over two more chairs for her and Gabe.

"I thought you weren't coming!" Brianna said, directing the question to her step-father.

"Change of heart!" Darrell replied.

He then waved his hand to his left to the dark-skinned, middle-aged black man and the dark-haired, green-eyed white woman beside him.

"I've brought friends I wanted Gabriel to meet!" Darrell continued.

Gabe looked over to the man and the woman that were seated beside Darrell. He noticed how the white woman kept smiling at him when Darrell introduced her as Trinity Sullivan and the man as George Warren. Brianna looked over at Gabe knowing he was about to say something.

"George Warren! Sharpshooter and best-known shot. You're labeled as the best shooter in the world!"

"You've heard of me?" George asked, smiling in approval at the young man.

"My grandfather was a fan!" Gabe admitted. "He was into guns and different types of weapons."

"How about you, boy?" George asked. "You also entertained by weapons?"

"I'm into making money!" Gabe told the guy, before looking over at Darrell. "Why am I meeting these people?"

Darrell listened to Gabe's question, but he then looked over to Lorenzo and nodded his head to him. Darrell waited as Lorenzo gathered the others and got them out of earshot. He then turned back to Gabe and Brianna.

"Here's the thing, Gabriel! Both George and Trinity are now your trainers. They will be training you for the work to come."

"Wait a minute!" Brianna spoke up. "You say training, huh? What's he need training for, Darrell? What aren't you telling us?"

"When the time comes, you both—!"

"Darrell!" Victoria interrupted, cutting off her husband and getting their attention. "Tell them!"

Darrell held his wife's eyes for a moment and then gave in to her demands. He looked back at both Gabe and Brianna.

"Do you remember the story we told you, Brianna, about how your father died?"

"Of course!"

"Well, we never told you that we knew who the killer was!"

"What?" Brianna yelled, looking over to her mother. "Is Darrell telling the truth?"

Victoria nodded her head yes.

"The same person that murdered your father, honey, is now locked up inside of a federal prison; but he is soon to be released in two years and he's coming here!"

"He's after you two, isn't he?" Gabe spoke up, asking Victoria but looking from her to Darrell and then back to her.

"Actually, Gabriel," Victoria began as she sat forward inside her seat, "he's after not only myself and Darrell, but also Brianna."

"Why me?" she asked.

Victoria began to explain to Brianna and Gabe how she and Darrell were the ones responsible for getting Brianna's father's killer locked up after setting him up and allowing the FBI to catch him in the middle of a cocaine buy.

"Wait!" Brianna spoke up after Victoria paused. "You say this person that killed my father was into buying cocaine?"

"Yes, sweetheart!" Victoria answered.

"But I thought my father was into robbing? Why would he have any dealings buying coke? I don't understand, Momma!"

Victoria sighed as she looked over at her husband and then continued. "Brianna, sweetie! Your father really wasn't into robbing. We only told you that to keep you away from this same lifestyle that you're already in. Your father was a very large cocaine distributor, and the same person who murdered him is or was your father's business partner!"

Gabe saw the expression on Brianna's face and reached over and gripped her hand.

"So let me get this clear. This person that's due to be released in two years, you say that he's after Brianna as well as the both of you. So, basically, I'm being trained to protect the three of you?"

"No!" Darrell spoke up again. "You two don't know it, but Lorenzo is around for the reason of protecting me and mostly Victoria. You're the one we've decided will protect Brianna; and seeing as though you two are now engaged, we figured you'll do whatever it takes to protect her and keep her safe."

Gabe nodded his head after listening to Darrell. He then shifted his eyes over to George and Trinity.

"I'm aware of what George Warren can do, but what about the white girl? What can you do, Trinity?"

"Be careful, Gabriel!" Victoria told him with a smile. "You may not know who Trinity is, but if you pull her up on the Internet you'll see what she's known for."

"How about somebody tell me!" Gabe requested, looking back over at Trinity.

"Trinity is the best mixed martial arts fighter in the world. She knows more than sixteen different fighting styles," Darrell explained to Gabe.

"And you're going to teach me all these styles?" Gabe asked as he looked back over at Trinity.

"I will attempt to teach you three styles to use," Trinity told him. "After seeing your ability with your hands, I can see you've fought already. Who showed you how to box?"

"My mother's father!" Gabe answered. "So, a'ight! We know the truth, so when does this training start?"

"You leave Monday morning, Gabriel,"

Darrell informed him.

"Whoa! What did you say?" Brianna asked, raising her voice. "What do you mean he's leaving? Where is my fiancé going?"

"We're leaving for Tokyo on Monday morning at 6:30 a.m.," Trinity spoke up.

"Naw!" Brianna interrupted. "Hell no! Y'all not taking my man across the fucking world to train him!"

"Bri, relax, ma!" Gabe told her, only for her to go off on him and refuse for him to go.

He leaned over and whispered into her ear a few moments. Gabe then pulled back and met her eyes. "Do you trust me?"

Brianna slowly shook her head, hating what he was asking her. She rolled her eyes and looked back over at Trinity.

"How long are you keeping him over there?"

"Depends on how fast a learner he is!" George answered this time. "I'll also be training Gabriel, so it can take from six to twelve months for him to really properly learn what he's being taught!"

"I can't believe this shit!" Brianna said, rolling her eyes in disgust.

Gabe watched Brianna for a few moments, until she looked back at him, and saw the look she gave him before taking his hand into hers. Gabe then winked at her and then looked back at Darrell and Victoria.

"We'll see you guys come Monday!"

To be continued . . .

Text Good2Go at 31996 to receive new release updates via text message.

To order books, please fill out the order form below:

*To order films please go to **www.good2gofilms.com***

Name:_____

Address:_____

City: _____ State: _____ Zip Code: _____

Phone:_____

Email:_____

Method of Payment: Check   VISA   MASTERCARD

Credit Card#:_____

Name as it appears on card: _____

Signature: _____

Item Name	Price	Qty	Amount
48 Hours to Die – Silk White	$14.99		
A Hustler's Dream - Ernest Morris	$14.99		
A Hustler's Dream 2 - Ernest Morris	$14.99		
Bloody Mayhem Down South	$14.99		
Business Is Business – Silk White	$14.99		
Business Is Business 2 – Silk White	$14.99		
Business Is Business 3 – Silk White	$14.99		
Childhood Sweethearts – Jacob Spears	$14.99		
Childhood Sweethearts 2 – Jacob Spears	$14.99		
Childhood Sweethearts 3 - Jacob Spears	$14.99		
Childhood Sweethearts 4 - Jacob Spears	$14.99		
Connected To The Plug – Dwan Marquis Williams	$14.99		
Connected To The Plug 2 – Dwan Marquis Williams	$14.99		
Deadly Reunion – Ernest Morris	$14.99		
Flipping Numbers – Ernest Morris	$14.99		
Flipping Numbers 2 – Ernest Morris	$14.99		
He Loves Me, He Loves You Not - Mychea	$14.99		
He Loves Me, He Loves You Not 2 - Mychea	$14.99		
He Loves Me, He Loves You Not 3 - Mychea	$14.99		
He Loves Me, He Loves You Not 4 – Mychea	$14.99		
He Loves Me, He Loves You Not 5 – Mychea	$14.99		
Lord of My Land – Jay Morrison	$14.99		
Lost and Turned Out – Ernest Morris	$14.99		
Loyalty To A Gangsta – J. L. Rose	$14.99		
Married To Da Streets – Silk White	$14.99		
M.E.R.C. - Make Every Rep Count Health and Fitness	$14.99		
Money Make Me Cum – Ernest Morris	$14.99		

My Besties – Asia Hill	$14.99		
My Besties 2 – Asia Hill	$14.99		
My Besties 3 – Asia Hill	$14.99		
My Besties 4 – Asia Hill	$14.99		
My Boyfriend's Wife - Mychea	$14.99		
My Boyfriend's Wife 2 – Mychea	$14.99		
My Brothers Envy – J. L. Rose	$14.99		
My Brothers Envy 2 – J. L. Rose	$14.99		
Naughty Housewives – Ernest Morris	$14.99		
Naughty Housewives 2 – Ernest Morris	$14.99		
Naughty Housewives 3 – Ernest Morris	$14.99		
Naughty Housewives 4 – Ernest Morris	$14.99		
Never Be The Same – Silk White	$14.99		
Slumped – Jason Brent	$14.99		
Someone's Gonna Get It - Mychea	$14.99		
Stranded – Silk White	$14.99		
Supreme & Justice – Ernest Morris	$14.99		
Supreme & Justice 2 – Ernest Morris	$14.99		
Supreme & Justice 3 – Ernest Morris	$14.99		
Tears of a Hustler - Silk White	$14.99		
Tears of a Hustler 2 - Silk White	$14.99		
Tears of a Hustler 3 - Silk White	$14.99		
Tears of a Hustler 4- Silk White	$14.99		
Tears of a Hustler 5 – Silk White	$14.99		
Tears of a Hustler 6 – Silk White	$14.99		
The Panty Ripper - Reality Way	$14.99		
The Panty Ripper 3 – Reality Way	$14.99		
The Solution – Jay Morrison	$14.99		
The Teflon Queen – Silk White	$14.99		
The Teflon Queen 2 – Silk White	$14.99		
The Teflon Queen 3 – Silk White	$14.99		
The Teflon Queen 4 – Silk White	$14.99		
The Teflon Queen 5 – Silk White	$14.99		
The Teflon Queen 6 - Silk White	$14.99		
The Vacation – Silk White	$14.99		

Tied To A Boss - J.L. Rose	$14.99		
Tied To A Boss 2 - J.L. Rose	$14.99		
Tied To A Boss 3 - J.L. Rose	$14.99		
Tied To A Boss 4 - J.L. Rose	$14.99		
Tied To A Boss 5 - J.L. Rose	$14.99		
Time Is Money - Silk White	$14.99		
Two Mask One Heart – Jacob Spears and Trayvon Jackson	$14.99		
Two Mask One Heart 2 – Jacob Spears and Trayvon Jackson	$14.99		
Two Mask One Heart 3 – Jacob Spears and Trayvon Jackson	$14.99		
Wrong Place Wrong Time – Silk White	$14.99		
Young Goonz – Reality Way	$14.99		
Subtotal:			
Tax:			
Shipping (Free) U.S. Media Mail:			
Total:			

Make Checks Payable To:
Good2Go Publishing
7311 W Glass Lane,
Laveen, AZ 85339

CPSIA information can be obtained
at www.ICGtesting.com
Printed in the USA
LVOW10s2202111017
552045LV00016B/315/P